A GIFT FOR CELESTINE

The village of St Justin is happy for archaeologist Alex to create a festival exhibition in the chateau beside the Dordogne. The highlight of the display is a fabulous necklace, a gift for a local girl who, centuries ago, was loved by the lord's son. But the jewels bring danger for Alex — and to brooding vineyard owner Raoul. Raw from past betrayals, he denies his attraction to her even as they are drawn closer. But Alex knows there can be no true love, no future, for them without trust . . .

SHEILA DAGLISH

A GIFT FOR
CELESTINE

Complete and Unabridged

LINFORD
Leicester

First published in Great Britain in 2020

First Linford Edition
published 2020

A catalogue record for this book is available
from the British Library.

ISBN 978–1–4448–4615–7

Published by
Ulverscroft Limited
Anstey, Leicestershire

Set by Words & Graphics Ltd.
Anstey, Leicestershire
Printed and bound in Great Britain by
T. J. International Ltd., Padstow, Cornwall

This book is printed on acid-free paper

1

The door almost left its hinges as the trio erupted into the bistro. Alex hid a smile as she watched.

In their early twenties, the women wore lightweight suits of sober grey and dark blue, which labelled them lunch-time refugees from one of the local banks.

'Ici, Monique! Voilà une table!' Laughing, they dumped wet umbrellas into the waiting stand before threading their way to the far corner. Despite the umbrellas, neither heads nor clothing had escaped the rain. Damp wisps clung to their flushed cheeks and it wasn't hard to imagine how glad they'd be to shake free their orderly coils of hair at the end of the day.

Wafer-thin as they were, they must be regular customers, thought Alex with an irrepressible glint of humour as she eyed the tiny square of gateau on her plate. *Marquise de chocolat* it said on the menu — but didn't add that it wouldn't detain her long!

La Tomate was more a salad bar than a restaurant, a few metres from the main thoroughfare and ideal for a light, easy lunch. It was still fairly empty and in the past she'd lingered here with a book and a coffee, watching the world pass by. Today, the sudden flurry of showers, typical of Provençal springtime, would with any luck soon move on, perhaps southwards across the lavender fields of southern France.

It was strange, this sense of having time to spare, and Alex wasn't sure that she liked it. It was even more unusual to be alone. Although she'd cherished occasional solitude, those hours had been rare and now she missed the camaraderie, the laughter and the sense of sharing. Patience was a virtue, she reminded herself, and the months would soon pass.

A fresh shower splattered the pavements, sending more customers inside for shelter and early lunch. The circular, wrought-iron tables with their spindly legs began to fill. A group of tourists, reaching for the menu, were casual in damp sun-tops and shorts, but most of the new arrivals, like the trio she'd first noticed, wore formal office clothes. Aix-en-Provence was a town of plane trees, elegant squares and dolphin fountains, a centre which successfully combined business with holidays and with education, a bustling, cosmopolitan mix which never failed to enchant her.

Head bent, Alex tackled the sticky mystery of her dessert, scarcely looking up when someone stopped beside her chair.

'You permit, mademoiselle?'

The newcomer, aged about fourteen, sounded hesitant, but spoke in English as she noticed the book propped open beside Alex's plate.

'Of course!' Alex's warm smile was

reassuring as, with a sigh of relief, the teenager sank into an empty chair on the far side of the table. Too young for college or university, she was probably approaching her final years of school but didn't project the natural confidence of someone used to town life. Her T-shirt was pretty, rather than trendy, her blue cotton jeans cinched with a plain leather belt.

The waitress, pony-tailed and pale-faced, in black tunic and tights, came after a few silent minutes in which Alex ate and read at the same time. The girl asked for a mineral water, explaining, 'My father will be here very soon and we will order our food then.'

The waitress nodded reluctantly, moving her thin frame and her order pad to a noisy cluster of students who were shuffling themselves around a larger table near the wall. The bistro was cramped, though not unpleasantly so and, despite opening directly onto the pavement, its whitewashed stone walls lent it the ambience of a bright and attractive cellar. Small deep-set windows allowed a view of the wet street and, although a neat splay of silk flowers was lodged on each slate window-ledge, there were real anemones and freesias in pottery jugs on every table.

Alex forked a final mouthful of dessert and brushed a smear of chocolate from her mouth with a hand tanned by months of Eastern sun. The girl on the far side of the table checked her watch. White and large, it swamped the sparrow-like bones of her wrist. From the way her fingers smoothed its broad leather strap and toyed with the elaborate dial, it was a prized, almost certainly new, acquisition.

The door opened again. Alex hoped the next comer would think to close it. There was a chill in the air and no heat inside the room. Tempting smells wafted from a square hatchway in the far wall, but the kitchen kept any warmth to itself.

Soon, the teenager's drink arrived.

Again she checked the entrance door, and then idly watched the street outside. Suddenly her eyes dilated.

'Oh, non!' Half-rising, she knocked her bead purse onto the floor. Diving to grab it, her agitation sent the purse skidding under the table.

Curious, Alex glanced through the window. What was all that about? There was nothing obvious outside. In fact, for these brief moments, the pavements were almost deserted. An old woman was shuffling along with a too-heavy basket of flowers, some children were sharing a bag of sweets, and a youngish man, head bent against a sudden squall, was hurrying towards Cours Mirabeau, the main promenade. No one was interested in La Tomate or its customers.

Alex's gaze returned to the girl. She was sitting lower, head bent, seemingly absorbed again in her wristwatch. It wasn't hard to guess that she'd prefer to stay on the floor with her purse.

Tempted to ask what had startled

her, Alex thought better of it. Those who knew her well often joked that she'd never learned to stay out of other people's troubles.

'Look how you always come off worst,' her friend Jenna had scolded when Alex stepped into a fight between two other girls at school. 'It was you who ended up with the bloodied nose!'

Alex went back to her book but it was no good — she couldn't resist another glance across the table. The child, for that's all she was, had straightened in her seat and now she smiled, albeit uncertainly.

Keeping one finger in the page she'd been reading, Alex returned the smile but then, resigned, closed the book. It was hard being a teenager, especially if you weren't one of the streetwise crew who'd think nothing of a solitary wait in unfamiliar surroundings. And something in the street had jolted, even upset this youngster.

'Are you on holiday?' she asked. 'This is such a beautiful town, it's no wonder so many visitors come to enjoy it.'

The other's eyebrows lifted behind her straggly fringe. She looked surprised by Alex's easy use of the local idiom.

'You are French? And from here, in the south?' Speaking in French, she cast a glance at Alex's book. 'I had thought you to be English.' Twisting her head to read the title page more clearly: 'Mary Stewart! It says this is another of her tales of Merlin and King Arthur. What could be more English than that?' A fleeting dimple appeared. Whatever the cause of her alarm, she had pulled herself into a semblance of calm.

'You're right about Arthur,' agreed Alex, amused. 'As for me, I'm half and half. My mother is French and my father was English. So I have a foot in both worlds.'

'I too, am half and half.' Looking oddly pleased that they shared a bond, the girl confided, 'Papa is French but my mother was American.'

'Was?' asked Alex gently.

'She died when I was three years old.' The words were matter-of-fact, and there was no doubting a mature acceptance of the reality, despite a momentary tightening of her lips.

'I'm sorry! I can imagine your sense of loss, even at that young age,' said Alex. 'My father collapsed and died ten years ago, when I was seventeen, but it seems like yesterday.' The familiar memory brought shadows to her face. For a moment, she was silent.

'It is different for me,' came the unexpected response. 'And maybe less difficult.' But then, perhaps disarmed by Alex's casual friendliness, and realising that her words sounded uncaring, she explained. 'It is sad, of course it is sad to have no mother, but I have Tante Marthe and funny little Tante Silvie. And it was so long ago.'

'Have you no memories of her at all?'

The girl shook her head, long brown hair swinging forward as she leaned to play with a leaf which had dropped from the tiny vase in the centre of the table.

'I have a faint memory of smooth chestnut-red hair and a musky perfume.' Wrinkling her nose, she looked up. 'I'm afraid it always makes me want to sneeze. I wonder if that is why I remember it!' Her smooth cheeks creased into laughter. It was a striking face, thought Alex. Beneath the fringe was a broad forehead, while wide-spaced hazel eyes and pointed chin lent elfin piquancy.

The gaze that met hers was straightforward.

'You must think me strange, unfeeling even. But I have been happy with only one parent.' A look, almost of surprise, crossed her face as though an alien emotion ruffled the surface of her words.

Alex didn't know what to say. This was so different from her own experience, the comfort she and her mother still drew from remembering the life and laughter they'd shared with her father. She struggled to find the right words.

Now a tinge of uncertainty crept into her companion's eyes as Alex stayed silent.

'Please forget what I said. I don't know what made me . . . '

'Don't worry.' Alex stretched out her hand and stilled the fingers that were tearing the tiny green leaf to shreds. 'I've sometimes found it easier to talk honestly with a stranger. You don't want to worry friends or family, and you're unlikely to meet the stranger again. There's no reason for them to repeat anything, so you've no need to watch your words.'

Her companion sank back, clearly relieved.

'You understand. Thank you!' As though shaking the conversation from her shoulders, she returned to Alex's earlier question, 'And no, I am not en vacances, but here for a short visit only.'

Her face brightened. 'My father has important business in Aix today.' She

11

couldn't suppress her excitement as she made the announcement. But then, her expression clouded once more.

Brows lifting, Alex wondered, *what now?*

The next confidence that came across the table was determinedly nonchalant. 'School is closed for Easter, so Papa said I could come with him. We arrived last night and shall leave tomorrow.' Again she glanced towards the door. Obviously he was late. 'Like you, I love this town. It is so bright and cheerful.'

'And full of students also,' added Alex, referring to the universities of this sunshine-clad region. 'My mother teaches History at university in Aix. She'd been happy in England but, once my father died, decided to come home and live near her relatives here in the south.' Mischief tilted her lips. 'Her vast and multi-layered network of relatives!'

The girl laughed. 'But what about you? Were you unhappy to leave your friends in England?'

Alex shook her head. 'No. My mother hadn't even expected to get an interview but when she was offered the post, we agreed she should come to France without me. I was settled at college, and it made sense to complete my exams, boarding on campus during term time.

'I'd known my career choice for ages, so when I was eventually accepted for the ideal course in Paris I was thrilled to bits! During vacations, I lived with my mother, just outside Aix, and found I liked being part of a large, lively family.'

Alex wondered about the teenager's own family. What were the two aunts like? Were they married, with children, all together in a community where a missing mother, a man's wife, had died? About to ask where they lived, she was interrupted.

The sun was blotted. out as a lithe, long-limbed man entered the cafe. His black brows were drawn together in a frown but eased as he sighted his daughter.

Her face lit as she turned and waved. 'Papa! Ici!' She swung back towards Alex with apologetic eyes. 'I beg your pardon. I hope you do not mind if my father joins us.'

Alex could hardly say no, because by now there were no empty tables, but she hoped the two of them would leave her to order coffee and finish her final chapter in peace.

'Papa' looked oddly out of place in this neat bistro with its low ceiling, elegant tables and menu which advertised a multitude of salads. Her own Salade Niçoise had been delicious, heaped with crisp green leaves, tomato, black olives and topped with a hot egg, but this man brought with him the heady tang of the outdoors. No genteel salad would suffice. He looked ready for steak and chips, or at the very least, a mound of rice topped by hearty coq au vin.

His frown returned as he asked 'You

permit, mademoiselle?'

The enquiry was so perfunctory that the renegade imp who often led Alex into trouble was tempted to retort, 'No, I'm waiting for my greatgrandmother and her toy-boy.'

Restraining herself, she indicated the vacant chair with an airy wave which brought a keen look and a hint of irritation to his lean features.

'I am sorry to be late, Lucie.' He touched the girl's shoulder with a light, sinewy hand as he sat. 'My meeting lasted for longer than intended.'

'And all is well?' The question was heavy with suspense, causing Alex to send a covert glance beneath her dark lashes. She wondered at their excitement. Why were they being so secretive?

With a swift look at Alex, who rapidly became engrossed in her book, he nodded.

'I think so.' He sighed. 'I certainly hope so. It was vital that we came today. And if we can produce something good ... ' He checked himself, but

Alex sensed an air of anticipation similar to his daughter's, but better concealed.

He was clean-shaven and, although strikingly masculine in a formal charcoal grey suit, she had a feeling he'd be more at ease wearing casual shirt and jeans, kerchief around his neck, cowboy or Romany-style. His dark hair curled untidily on his brow, while swarthy skin, hawklike nose and high cheekbones hinted that his roots lay in the Camargue. There, on the salt flats, where small black bulls and white horses roamed beneath a flamingo-pink sky, he'd relax — not here, in a busy town and trendy bistro!

Her mind flew to the exotic gypsies she'd seen leaving the dusty boulevard in Aries for their annual pilgrimage to Les Saintes Marie de la Mer. The men, dark-eyed, at one with the earth; their women, in swirling skirts of orange, red, purple, a vibrant spectacle. Once the coffin of Sarah, servant of Mary Magdalene, had been lowered, and later raised above the church altar, they'd return to their never-ending travels. Yes, he'd be completely at home among them.

Another glance left Alex wondering. He didn't seem like a man who'd be without a woman for long. And yet Lucie hadn't mentioned one.

'I thought I saw . . . ' Lucie fell silent, obedient to the silent command. There was a sombre air about him, at odds with the gentleness he showed his daughter. But then, reassured by Alex's absorption in her book, she whispered, 'I think we were almost too late.'

Nodding, his hand brushed her cheek.

'No, we were just in time. But only just!'

The waitress brought Alex's coffee and stood, notebook poised and eyes alert to the man's slightest wish. Risking another covert look. Alex decided that, although Lucie's father wasn't handsome, he had a masculine appeal that would be hard to withstand if he also possessed charm. Just for now, she hadn't spotted any. His black eyes had been cold and indifferent when they met hers, a reaction which, she acknowledged ruefully, wasn't what she was accustomed to.

Father and daughter were silent, a silence which was particularly notice-able after the casual conversation he'd interrupted. It was clear that Lucie recognised his reluctance to talk about the business meeting where others might overhear.

Alex took pity on her discomfort.

'Would you like this? You can keep it until after you've eaten.' She proffered the sugar-coated bonbon which had arrived with her coffee. 'I think the patron meant it as an apology for the size of his marquise.' Her smiling eyes were directed to the youngster, ignoring the man beside her.

'Thank you. You are kind. And probably correct!' Lucie giggled as she cast a glance at Alex's empty plate. After a few minutes, in an obvious attempt to renew the former easy atmosphere, she asked, 'May I look at your book, mademoiselle?'

'Of course!' Alex pushed it towards her. She had reached the last few pages but there was no chance of enjoying it until she left this small restaurant. If the showers held off, she might visit the market as she'd planned. On the other hand, it could be pleasant to drink another, solitary, uninterrupted coffee beneath the plane trees which were already beginning to unfurl their buds. Soon the streets would be sheltered by a canopy of leaves, salvation when summer was at its height and the heat could be hard to bear. Heat! She was used to that, not to mention the discomfort it could bring!

Lucie was reading the inscription on the flyleaf. '*For Alex, in hope that this book might tempt her and her trowel to England. Much love, Mike.*'

'Your trowel? Pardon, mademoiselle. My father insists that we often speak English at home, but my vocabulary is poor. Ask him!' She flashed the man a cheeky look.

'The problem isn't with your language skills, Lucie,' said Alex, twisting the book to remind herself of the inscription. 'It's more to do with my friend's sense of humour. He's always persuading me to apply for a job in England, where he's employed for the foreseeable future.'

'But why bring your 'trowel'?' Lucie's forehead puckered.

'It means just that!' She saw the girl's puzzlement and went on to explain. 'I work as an archaeologist. For several years I've specialised in the East, and have been fortunate enough to dig in countries such as Egypt and Jordan. Firstly as a student, and now as a full member of the team.' She couldn't hide the glow of satisfaction in her deep blue eyes as she added, 'I've just returned from a spell in The Valley of the Kings.'

Lucie's father, a dark and silent presence, had ordered his lunch which arrived quickly and, true to her prediction, turned out to be steak and pommes frites, accompanied by a bowl of tossed salad. Pouring red wine from the carafe which the waitress set beside him, he swallowed a mouthful as if he needed it, although his lips pursed as he viewed his glass with a jaundiced eye. Abruptly, as though he couldn't contain his interest, he looked directly at Alex.

'The Valley of the Kings?' he repeated. 'A fascinating area for study of the past, but the work must be hard.'

'Yes. And hot!'

'Forgive me, but you seem hardly the type for such labour.' His comprehensive look swept Alex's tangle of golden curls and the delicate bones of a face which held a tantalising hint of humour and character, alongside sun-kissed cheeks and freckled nose. It was a face that any man would look at twice, and he did this before his eyes moved to the slim, almost boyish, figure clad in white cropped jeans and a strappy blue sun-top which revealed tanned arms and shoulders. His eyes were thoughtful as they strayed to her hands, smooth but capable, the fingernails short, coated in clear varnish.

'I'm tougher than I look,' Alex assured him briskly, not altogether pleased by the cool inspection, the hint of disbelief in his tone and the scepticism in his eyes.

Something that was nearly a smile touched one corner of his mouth, although it vanished so quickly that Alex wondered if she'd imagined it. A frisson, almost of recognition, ran up her spine.

'I am sure you are.'

The response was so obviously placatory that, not having expected any humour in him, she burst out laughing.

The expression on his face changed. Dark eyes alert, he seemed to be looking at her for the first time, despite his earlier almost insolent appraisal.

'Eat up, your lunch is getting. cold,' she reminded him in a tone that echoed his own but had a hint of starchy nursemaid.

'Yes, ma'am!' he drawled in a passable American accent.

Lucie was listening to this by-play, and it was apparent that she was astounded to hear her father so relaxed with a stranger.

'Are you soon to return to Egypt, mademoiselle?'

Her attempt to prolong the conversation accompanied an almost apologetic glance at her father but he was still watching Alex as though, despite himself, he was interested in her answer.

Alex sighed. 'No — not yet, at any rate. The permit for this season's dig has expired and we're waiting for permission to return when the time's right. Until then, we have to down tools and make ourselves scarce.' She and Lucie had continued talking in a mixture of French and English, and although the teenager occasionally frowned at a word or phrase, she understood the gist.

'May I ask in which part of France

you live?' Alex addressed the man who had returned to his meal and resumed eating with the air of someone who had breakfasted many hours ago. 'Lucie told me that you are here just for the day, on business.'

He swallowed the last of his steak and, pushing the plate aside, raised a finger for the waitress to bring coffee. By now, Lucie had devoured a Caesar salad, and asked for creme caramel.

'We live in the Dordogne region, within tolerable reach of the town of Sarlat,' he told Alex. 'Do you know the area?'

Alex's eyes brightened. Clear, tilted almost with a hint of the Orient, and fringed by dark lashes, they were particularly striking against the rich colouring of her hair. 'Yes, I've spent several holidays there with an old schoolfriend, Jenna de Villiers. The last time was about three years ago. Her aunt and uncle own a very old inn in a riverside village named St Justin.'

'I know it and, of course its crowning

glory, the chateau.'

'Chateau of the Nymph, as romantic as its name,' remembered Alex.

'Perhaps you will visit there again.'

Was there a note in his voice that indicated he wouldn't be averse to the idea? Mentally she slapped herself. This wasn't a man seeking women's company. There was a remoteness about him. He meant to maintain his distance.

Lucie had no such reticence.

'It would be lovely to see you there, mademoiselle. If we give you our telephone number, perhaps you would let us know if you plan to be in St Justin.'

Without waiting for her father's assent, she scribbled some figures on the white table napkin and pushed it across to Alex.

Although doubting that she would ever use the number, Alex thanked her and felt obliged to add, 'If I'm ever that way and you answer the phone, I'd better tell you that my name is Alex Graham.'

'Alex? A boy's name.' It was the man who spoke.

'Alexandrie really, but that's a bit of a mouthful if someone's yelling, *Shift yer butt, give us the wheelbarrow!*'

Again his mouth quirked, as though long ago it had known how to smile.

'I see the problem, although it's a pity to shorten so charming a name.' Despite the compliment, he gave no indication that he, unlike his daughter, would like to renew their acquaintance.

Alex felt a slow flush that had nothing to do with the increasing warmth of the bistro as sunshine finally filtered through the windows. Whether intentional or not, he did have charm, and used it almost carelessly. Even so, she couldn't imagine herself telephoning the family home — but Lucie was looking at her father, expecting him to return the courtesy.

'My name is Raoul Giravel of La Petite Grotte vineyard. And this is Lucie, of course.'

His detachment was a subtle challenge. *Remember us if you dare!* Doubtless he'd prefer to remain incognito, thought Alex, unusually piqued.

Pushing aside his chair and rising to go, Raoul extended his hand. His hard fingers closed around hers and a feeling of rightness made her stay, trapped within his clasp, while their eyes met.

She knew he sensed it too from the fleeting expression, almost of regret, behind his unsmiling gaze. Raoul Giravel was dangerous — a man who could threaten upheaval in her orderly world.

Lucie came around the table and, instead of offering her hand, kissed Alex on both cheeks.

'Thank you Alex, I hope we meet again. I shall not forget you.'

And then they were gone.

Once they had turned the corner and were out of sight, Alex felt oddly bereft. Berating herself for idiotic fantasies, she paid her bill and left.

An hour or so spent in the market

beneath the wide steps of the Palais de Justice was always fun. The kaleidoscope of colours, perfumes, and the bonhomie of stall holders almost hidden behind pyramids of fruit and vegetables, cheeses, stacks of books, antiques and bric-a-brac was endlessly fascinating. And then the cool calm of the Cathedral invariably beckoned. The historians had finished their work, so that ancient paintings and worn stone carvings rested in the shadows once more, reminders of the town's men and women, dissolved now into history.

Eventually she retraced her steps to the crowded Rue Cardinale, where cars jostled for space beside the narrow pavement.

A ten-minute drive took Alex to her mother's home, a compact stone cottage with peach-coloured roof-tiles and creamy roughcast walls. Eloise was enjoying a cool drink in her favourite place, a rough-timbered terrace entwined with fragrant creepers and overlooked by the towering white-grey mountain beloved by the artist Cezanne. She looked at her daughter's wind-blown hair without surprise.

'I can see you had the hood down.'

Alex laughed. 'Guilty!'

She loved her small blue runabout and, despite the sometimes sharp air of early spring, invariably kept the top lowered, muttering when she had to stop, jump out and snap it into place when the showers came.

Wandering into the kitchen, she opened the refrigerator, and then, carrying a jug of iced lemonade, joined Eloise in the dappled shade outside. Sinking into a comfortable basket chair, she casually mentioned Lucie and the fact that the Giravel family lived in the Dordogne area.

'I don't remember the name Giravel but then I'm not really familiar with that region,' said Eloise. She pushed back a stray lock of dark brown hair, escaping from the casual knot she wore at home, and which miraculously became a neat chignon when she left the house each day and drove to the university.

Alex's mother was in her late forties but still possessed the figure of someone far younger. Her hair and complexion were completely different from her daughter, whose fiery golden locks had been inherited from her father. The two striking features Alex shared with Eloise were dark blue eyes and the hint of sweetness around a mouth which seemed to tilt upwards even when life was occasionally grey.

Eloise frowned slightly, trying to visualise the course of the Dordogne river to where it eventually flowed into the sea.

'Their property can't be far from St Justin, where you used to stay with Jenna at the inn.' She looked enquiringly at Alex. 'Have you heard recently from her?'

Eloise liked Alex's tall, fair-haired friend. The girls had met at school in England and then shared a room at college. Later, their paths had diverged. Jenna pursued a degree in art and design, while Alex, whose first love had always been ancient history and archaeology, found her ideal course in France.

'A card and a scribble at Christmas.' Alex topped up her drink and sipped it with a sigh of pleasure as she wriggled more comfortably into the chair and propped her sandalled feet on the low magazine rack. 'She's ecstatically happy with Luc and they're expecting a second baby in a few months. They live in Paris for most of the year but of course Luc has to make frequent visits to St Justin because of the chateau.'

'That old building and the rest of the estate will be a burden on Luc's shoulders until Guy is old enough to take over,' said Eloise thoughtfully, referring to Luc's young nephew. 'Always assuming the boy will want to leave Paris. He'll be a young man by then.'

'Yes, though he loves the chateau and knows it's the family's ancestral home.

His mother has made a success of her computer company so he's getting a good education, but, even so, I daresay money is tight. It might be hard for them to up sticks and eventually move to St Justin.'

Alex didn't refer again to Lucie, nor mention the girl's father. She knew the interpretation that Eloise, hoping to see her daughter settled in France, would place on the lunchtime meeting with an enigmatic Frenchman. It had been more a sparring match than a conversation, thought Alex. Unwillingly, too, she knew she'd enjoyed it.

With an effort, she turned the talk to the family wedding which she and Eloise would be attending in a few weeks.

Nonetheless, her thoughts often strayed during the next few days. Raoul Giravel was a man she would have liked to know better.

She'd had casual men-friends since university days, one of them being Mike Delaney, who had given her the Merlin book. As students, they'd worked on digs both in England and France, until Alex was offered the chance to go to Egypt.

Mike telephoned from England one evening.

'Hi, Alex! Thanks for your email. Sorry your dig couldn't get an extension permit just yet.' He sounded in high spirits and listened with genuine interest as Alex described some of the triumphs and frustrations her team had encountered.

When she asked about his own work, Mike, as always, tried to tempt her to join an excavation on which he'd been working for several weeks.

'It's near the Scottish border — shades of Hadrian's Wall and all that. But we've come across domestic artefacts in an area no one had previously dug.' His voice dropped into shades of mock-seduction. 'There might be a patch of soil, or even a ditch, for you, too! We've plenty of keen amateurs but there's a lot going on elsewhere so, unusually, we're short of professionals.'

For a moment Alex was tempted. She could do with the money, if there really was a space on the team, now the Middle East project had ground to a temporary halt. In any case, common sense said she should keep up-to-date with work going on in Europe.

Against that, did she want to spend time with Mike? She liked him hugely as a friend, but he'd made no secret about wishing to become closer. Was it fair to let him hope she might start wanting that too? Surely she should feel a spark, a tingle of attraction?

'I won't make any promises, Mike,' she said eventually. 'But thanks for the suggestion. I'll admit I'm wondering if it's right to think exclusively of long-distance work. My mother never tries to stop me but I know she'd love me to be closer-either France, or just a Channel-hop away.'

Reluctantly Mike accepted that Alex wouldn't give an immediate answer, and rang off, protesting such undying love that she burst into laughter, relieved when he joined in.

She had scarcely put down the receiver when the phone rang again.

'Alex!' It was Jenna. 'Thank heaven you're there! We've a massive problem and I need you. At the chateau!'

2

Jenna sounded so stressed that Alex's smile fled.

'What's wrong? Is the baby all right? Or is it Michel?'

'No, my bump is fine, and so is Michel, though he must soon learn to share his toys.' Jenna's voice dropped almost to its normal level, although she couldn't hide her worry. 'But we're in a dreadful fix. Please say you'll help.'

'Jenna — explain!' Alex perched on the telephone stool. This could take some time. 'How did you know I was here? I sent you a postcard of a pyramid — or perhaps it was a desert — less than a month ago.'

'And it has pride of place on my mantelpiece, I swear,' Jenna assured her. 'Alongside all the other postcards of pyramids and deserts you've sent!' Laughing, and starting to recover her usual composure, she said, 'If I had any psychic powers, they've certainly deserted me now. Probably shock at being pregnant again, before Michel's second birthday.

'No, there's nothing supernatural about it. You might be surprised that I heard news of your presence from a rather gorgeous man who lunched with you in Aix last week.'

Alex blinked. 'Raoul Giravel?' She'd thought it unlikely that he would spare her more than a passing thought, if even that, once he'd walked out of the bistro and out of her life.

'The same. He's an old friend of Luc's. We're at the chateau for a couple of days and I saw Raoul yesterday, coming out of the bank in Sarlat. I suppose that, having met you recently, he was struck by the coincidence, since you'd mentioned that we're friends.'

Alex wanted to ask more but was still trying to frame a casual question when Jenna went on, 'Apparently you were a big hit with his daughter, Lucie.'

'Was Lucie with him?' Alex asked, aware that her heartbeat had quickened at the thought of the black-browed man who had almost, just almost, held her hand for longer than was necessary.

'No, he said she was at school. We had a quick lunch. The food was superb!' Jenna's reminiscent sigh made Alex wonder just how quick the lunch had, in truth, been. She'd always teased Jenna about her appetite and bewailed the fact that somehow her friend stayed as slim as a reed.

'He was asking about you,' Jenna added, as though she would never dream of matchmaking for anyone, let alone Alex.

'Was he?' Alex struggled, but managed to sound only vaguely interested. 'That's nice.'

'Surprising, at any rate. He's steered clear of women since losing his wife. He seems to have an almighty hang-up about letting anyone else get close.' Delicately, she added, 'You could be just the girl to change all that.'

Alex ignored her. 'I gathered from Lucie that her mother died some years ago.'

'Yes, I believe Lucie was a toddler. Raoul never let on, but Luc heard from an American business pal that the wife had a weakness for handsome men, so the marriage may have hit the rocks anyway, given time. I think there was some sort of money problem too, but didn't want to pry.' Jenna sounded amused. 'Luc would never admit it, but men are worse gossips than women!'

'Lucie obviously gets on well with her father,' said Alex. 'Apparently she's been brought up by two aunts.' Despite herself, she couldn't resist fishing in the dark waters of Raoul Giravel's life, wanting to know more about him, but determined not to ask. 'Lucie sounded happy, so there's been no desperate need for a stepmother,' she added firmly.

'Perhaps.' Jenna didn't sound convinced. 'Anyway, we're wandering from my crisis.'

'What crisis?'

'Luc and I have a situation you might describe as dire. What we want to know is — for how long will you be in France this time? Or have you already packed your bag, ready to dash off East again?'

'My work out East is temporarily at a standstill, but Mike thinks there might be something for me in England, along the Northumberland borders.'

'Mike Delaney?' Jenna sounded exasperated. 'He never gives up, does he?'

'The same. And no, he doesn't.'

'In that case, you're hired! Luc and I urgently need you at the chateau.'

'What's the problem?' asked Alex cautiously. She'd had previous experience of Jenna's schemes, which invariably led to Alex metaphorically putting her head in the lion's jaws.

'Well, as you know, the estate at St Justin is desperate for cash, so we've opened the grotto beneath the building as a tourist attraction. At the same time, we decided it made sense to create a small museum.'

'Displaying the necklace.'

'Yes, it's only a replica, of course. The gems found in the grotto are priceless, so the real necklace is in Paris under decent security.'

Alex already knew the story. A fabulous necklace from the Orient had been hidden for centuries in the forgotten grotto. Her imagination had spun a web of romance around the tragedy of the lord's son. Marcel had ridden with Richard the Lionheart in his Crusade to win Jerusalem from its Saracen defenders. They didn't succeed but Marcel escaped with the wonderful necklace. Returning home, he found that his father had died and he was now lord of the chateau.

By now Alex had abandoned the stool and was sitting on the tiled floor, her back to the wall, tanned legs stretched out in front of her. She thought back to when she last visited the great stone fortress, playing with the little boy, Guy, and lunching al fresco in the sunshine with Jenna and Luc, her husband.

'I remember Marcel brought back the jewels for Celestine, the innkeeper's daughter,' Alex said slowly. 'She'd given birth to Marcel's son while he was away, then the rumour spread that he was to marry an heiress. Believing the story, Celestine drowned herself and her child in the Dordogne.'

'That's right,' said Jenna. 'Marcel was devastated. He hid the necklace in the grotto where they used to meet secretly. Then he had that fantastic marble statue erected in the courtyard.'

Alex recalled the poignant, ethereal figure, looking eastwards, Celestine eternally waiting.

'And that's how it got its name, Chateau de la Nymphe, of course. So what's the current crisis?'

A heavy sigh came down the phone line.

'Two days ago, Gertrud, our curator, had an urgent message from Switzerland. Her mother is terminally ill and, naturally, it's essential that Gertrud is with her.'

Alex was beginning to see where Jenna's explanation was leading. Jenna hurried on.

'The huge difficulty is that, whereas normally I could have taken over, and kept Michel with me — he's a very accommodating little boy — this latest pregnancy is throwing up complications and it's likely that I'll be hospitalised for a while. So . . . '

'You want me to fill in. For the main tourist season — basically the whole summer.'

'You've got it in one!' Jenna paused and Alex, knowing her friend well, waited. There had to be a catch. There was.

'There's one more difficulty, and that's why we must have someone who knows her history from start to finish.'

'What I know about the Crusades or precious jewels could be packed inside a matchbox.'

'Don't worry, you can soon swot up on them,' came the ruthless reply. 'Our main headache is that this year is the anniversary of the founding of St Justin centuries ago, when a simple friar arrived and lived in a cave, preaching. The council want a big celebration, with the real necklace on show, to draw visitors and do wonders for the local economy. So it's essential to have a personable, articulate, professional historian running the museum.'

Alex ignored the blatant flattery.

'What do I do? Sit beside the gems every night with a shotgun?'

'Something like that!' A peal of laughter came all the way from Paris. 'No, you nutter, of course not! There'll be extra security, even a couple of guards. You won't have a thing to worry about.'

Eventually, despite reservations, because things with Jenna were never as simple as they appeared on the surface, Alex knew she would probably agree. A few weeks in St Justin meant she'd be in an idyllic location where her mother could join her during the university vacation, it would help

Jenna and Luc, and might solve the problem of how to keep Mike Delaney at a distance without hurting his feelings.

Having sown the seeds of the solution, Jenna decided it expedient to chat about life in Paris and the expected baby, and then wanted news of Alex's latest dig and old college friends.

'How is your Aunt Elspeth — and Uncle Philippe, of course?'

Alex was fond of Jenna's aunt and uncle. They had first made her welcome on childhood holidays in the village and then, after Jenna and Luc's wedding, she'd spent a few days with them when the newlyweds went on honeymoon.

'They're blooming, especially now Philippe's cousin is doing their admin,' said Jenna. 'As Luc and I are often in St Justin, we've been able to keep an eye on them.'

Already, Alex accepted that she was committed. She was the obvious choice and, more to the point, was available.

Luc, a successful architect, was financially independent but after his older brother, Hugo, drowned in a yachting accident, Luc and Madeleine, his brother's wife, had fought to safeguard the estate. Otherwise, Hugo's young son, Guy, would inherit an empty title and a gigantic millstone around his neck.

There could be no question of selling Celestine's necklace, such an intrinsic part of the de Villiers history — but, with its help, they might raise extra income by making use of the anniversary celebrations.

Alex knew she had to help. She'd been a sitting duck, she realised with a grin.

The conversation came to a halt at last. Silence. Then, cautiously from the Paris end of the phone line:

'So you'll do it?'

'OK, OK, I'll do it!' Ignoring Jenna's shriek of relief, Alex said, 'I'll enjoy seeing your aunt and uncle again, and, to be honest, it'll be a comfort to have friends close at hand if I run into trouble.'

At that point Jenna had to say goodbye.

'Michel's just woken up, so I must go. But I'll see you soon at the chateau. Luc and I plan to be there next week. I can't tell you what a weight you've taken off our shoulders. You're a star!'

3

Two days, later, Alex set off for the village of St Justin in her beloved car, the hood down as usual. Eloise had been quietly, but obviously, delighted that her daughter would be in France for a few months. She would join Alex once the term's teaching commitments came to an end.

The day was dry and warm as Alex drove away from the pine-clad foothills and grey-white ridges of the Mont St Victoire, onward through the noisy streets of Aix. All too soon the air lost that heady scent of orange-blossom which signalled home. Leaving the dramatic outlines of the south, as she travelled northwards the land became gently undulating until the great curves of the Dordogne meandered in lazy sweeps ahead of her.

It was quite a long drive and, without

the need to hurry, Alex stayed overnight in the village of Villeclos, which she knew as a convenient staging-post between north and south, and one with a comfortable auberge and restaurant that, she'd recalled, served wonderful escargots heaving with hot garlic oil.

What a pig you've become, Alex Graham. But what a treat to eat without crunching sand between your teeth! All the same, she sighed. She'd loved her job and was missing it.

Leaving early next morning, she felt the first real tingle of anticipation. What would the next few months bring? Despite an initial reluctance to take on Jenna's project, she knew herself well enough to guess that she'd enjoy what sounded like a refreshingly different career track. *Something to add to my CV*, she thought, amused.

Nearing the main street of St Justin, Alex could see the chateau rearing high, as if stretching to touch the few tufty white clouds which drifted in a clear blue sky.

Beneath it, within a hundred metres of the river, a single line of medieval buildings had, years ago, been carved into the limestone rock-face. Nowadays they were mostly cafes, bars, souvenir shops, although there was still a boulangerie and a general store which sold everything from candles to cabbages, tin openers to clothes pegs.

From street level, narrow steps and alleys led upwards to a terrace which lodged more small houses, some just crumbled ruins and deserted vegetable patches. Where the terrace divided, one path led to a lichen-covered fountain almost hidden by trees. The other path sloped upwards to the yellow-grey stone walls which had once protected the lord of the manor.

The main entrance of the chateau was open as Alex negotiated the tight hairpin bends from her route alongside the river. Beyond wrought-iron gates stretched a gravelled courtyard.

There, overlooking the battlements, the weather-stained white marble statue of a nymph stood poised, as if to fly.

'Celestine, still waiting and hoping,' murmured Alex as she swung between the wide gates. The delicate figure had always intrigued her and its tragic history inevitably still breathed a world of romance.

She hardly had time to switch off the engine before the carved oak door of the building swung open and a petite, black-clad figure hurried down the wide steps to greet her.

'Madame Dupont! It's good to see you again!' Alex had known the little woman since childhood. Now in her seventies, the housekeeper occupied comfortable quarters here, but it was a standing joke that she wouldn't dream of missing her daily excursions to friends along the river bank, returning with more local news than any official journal could gather.

Critically Madame Dupont assessed Alex as she slid from the driving seat and stooped to kiss each lined cheek, lines which deepened firstly into a smile and then grew severe.

'What is this?' She looked Alex up and down, unimpressed by the casual sun-top and matching green shorts. 'You are skin and bone! What do you eat? Lettuce leaves?' Scolding, she ushered Alex into the main entrance hall.

Its size and lofty vaulted ceiling made the room impractical for everyday use, and now housed enough antiques to transform it into a small museum. Alex knew that, as soon as she'd unpacked, she would take a look at the few glass cabinets along the walls. Probably they held the replica necklace and other family mementoes. Already she was visualising the great hall as a focal point for the exhibition.

The stone walls were hung with a few portraits but mostly landscapes, probably recent purchases to cover blank spaces. Financial strain must have forced previous generations of the family to sell prized paintings and heirlooms.

Alex sighed. Even if the estate became solvent again, the bulk of any cash must repair properties housing tenants and the land they cultivated. Refurbishment of the main building to its original grandeur would have to come last.

The housekeeper hurried her towards the spacious, high-raftered kitchen, always the family's favourite gathering place.

'I remember how, even as a child, you loved your cup of coffee!' Madame Dupont filled the kettle and took out cups, saucers, a strawberry flan and sugar-dusted sponge cake. 'You are too thin, all you young women,' she said again. 'Just see what a difference there will be, once you have enjoyed some home cuisine!'

Fervently hoping her clothes would still fit by the end of summer, Alex meekly accepted a slice of flan and let the housekeeper do her worst with the jug of cream.

Soon, she was led upstairs to a

charming bedroom and sitting-room with adjoining bathroom.

'Madame Jenna said you will need privacy to relax and plan for the. hundreds of visitors who will pay to come,' the housekeeper announced.

'Have there been many visitors since the museum was opened?'

'But certainement! There was great excitement, of course, when the magnificent necklace was discovered, just beneath where we stand now.' Madame Dupont swooped her arms so eloquently that Alex's eyes were drawn to the floor.

'Reporters came from newspapers and television. We did not like them asking questions because it meant we must talk again about Monsieur Hugo's sad death. But of course it made a good story for them, one that would sell. Madame Madeleine left her son at home in Paris, but now they often visit here.'

'Madeleine must have been so anxious to shield Guy,' said Alex, imagining the young mother's stress. Already she must have realised that, if they could open the grotto to visitors and inside the chateau create a fascinating museum, its centrepiece the necklace, the estate might survive — and even prosper.

'He is only ten years old,' agreed the housekeeper. 'But perhaps one day he will live at the chateau — who knows? All we can do is earn money to make it great again.'

Privately Alex doubted it would achieve such heights, but as an appealing venue on the tourist map, the new exhibition should help.

You'd better make a good job of it, Alexandrie Graham, she thought.

Tired from two days of driving, despite her midway overnight stop, she couldn't keep back a tiny yawn soon after the hearty cassoulet which Madame Dupont considered a light supper.

In her room she watched as moonlight illuminated the battlements and glinting distant waters. She visualised Richard, French-born and bred yet king of England, riding through towns and villages to recruit Crusaders, and then, after his captivity, returning from the East with little to show but his new title, Lionheart.

Caught up in the magic of the night, she imagined Marcel, too, his blood afire with the spirit of adventure. Eventually, coming home, he knew he was expected to marry well, an alliance that must come before love. But what promises had he made to his secret sweetheart? Had Celestine, even as he rode away, suspected she might be pregnant? If so, she'd said nothing, but been obliged to let him go.

Earlier, Alex had carried her suitcase upstairs and slung her belongings on the bed. Now, a folded paper slid from her shoulder bag. Her lips curved as she recognised the napkin on which Lucie had scrawled the Giravel telephone number. There was small chance she'd ever use it!

Her head told her to throw it in the bin but her heart said otherwise. Silly really, just a tiny keepsake of the hour she'd spent with Raoul Giravel. Fascinating, withdrawn, but a man who'd disturbed her senses with the fleeting touch of his hand.

Deriding herself for her own weakness, she tucked the napkin back inside the bag. *Dream on, you idiot!* With a sigh, Alex slid beneath the bed covers and slept.

⋆ ⋆ ⋆

Next morning, she awoke at dawn. Reluctant to draw the curtains last night, she'd invited early sunshine to stream across the faded carpet. Dragging on jeans and warm fleece, within minutes she was outdoors, leaning over the battlements, looking to where the village was beginning to stir. A few delivery vans were disgorging their loads, and waiters were sweeping around open-air tables before they donned white aprons ready to serve breakfast of coffee and warm, crispy rolls.

From here, she couldn't quite see the mellow rooftops of the Auberge des Fleurs, where Jenna's aunt and uncle would be starting their day. She was looking forward to visiting them later.

Firstly though, she must walk around, viewing the chateau with the critical appraisal of ticket-paying visitors. What would they expect to see? What improvements could she make on whatever Gertrud had already set up? As for events celebrating the centuries-old arrival of St Justin, the preacher, Jenna and Luc would know what, so far, had been planned.

The main door was unlocked, as she half-expected. It was a sure bet that Madame Dupont was an early riser. Perhaps expecting Alex to sleep on after the long drive, all was quiet, so she was free to make a silent assessment of this, her summertime task.

Mentally purchasing a ticket at a

small, new-looking kiosk, she walked up the steps and into the great hall. At the far end, a wide stone staircase led upwards, around it a gallery overlooking an enormous marble fireplace, flagstoned floor and a few glass-topped showcases.

Leaning on the balustrade, Alex peered from the gallery. She screwed up her nose. As curator, Gertrud hadn't shown much imagination although, to be fair, she'd been faced with a blank canvas.

The imitation necklace looked insignificant, when it should be the main showstopper. Alex had once seen the original stones and remembered their unique fire, generating such life that no one could possibly forget their romantic history. How to do them justice?

Discreet spotlights, from each corner, she decided, *And spread the gems on a bed of dark velvet. I'll try that, just for starters!*

Slowly descending the stairs, she murmured, 'Colour — that's what this place needs.' Viewing the hall from each corner, eyes half-closed, she felt a tingle of excitement. *Not flowers, but flags, banners, heraldic pennants. And what about* . . . Imagination took flight and, by the time she had finished a breakfast of coffee, croissants and Madame Dupont's apricot conserve in the kitchen, her notebook was a riot of rough sketches and scribbled ideas.

Soon she was exploring again. The library walls, lined with shelves, were reasonably well-stocked with books, although none looked particularly old or valuable. Presumably the original volumes had been sold.

Pen in hand, she tapped her bottom lip, lost in thought. Another display would add interest here. What about an illustrated history — the earliest building, the story of Marcel, the young medieval lord and his secret love, the village girl, Celestine?

Thoughtfully she tried to visualise the sweethearts' world, the Crusaders' hopes and how the wreckage of those dreams had devastated lives and love. What about borrowing or hiring maps, costumes and anything else that would bring to life the journey through lands that had ultimately led to Jerusalem?

'We could have full-size figures in battle wear,' she breathed, already thinking how best to track some down. Eyes sparkling, she couldn't wait to get started.

There was still no sign of Madame Dupont, so Alex drank another coffee before going outside with her notes and sketchpad. The arched doorway to the keep was unlocked and, inside, steep steps led down to the grotto. The mouth of the entrance tunnel yawned black and cavernous.

Deciding to leave it for now, she retraced her steps, reluctant to tamper with Luc's temporary lantern system. Once the buildings were opened to the public, the great crystal cave would be properly illuminated.

She remembered her first visit there, with Luc and Jenna. Then, there were only a few cables stringing lightbulbs together. Even so, it had seemed lit by a thousand stars.

There would be time to explore, but her first job was to work some magic in the museum, a sleeping chrysalis, soon to be a vibrant butterfly!

With a lot of luck! Alex thought, pulling a face.

In the afternoon she walked down the rough stone alleyway to the Auberge des Fleurs.

'Alex! How lovely to see you! Jenna rang to say you'd soon be in St Justin again.' Elspeth, Jenna's aunt, hugged her.

Single until her early forties, she had met and fallen in love with Philippe, marrying and moving to France at such speed her family were left breathless. Trim and smiling, she had greying brown curls and the air of a woman contented with her life.

Over coffee in the workmanlike kitchen which catered for their often-busy restaurant, Elspeth agreed the museum left much to be desired.

'Gertrud is a nice young woman, a worthy soul, you might say. But I never credited her with original thinking. Philippe thought the same.'

Her husband had entered the room, and set down a loaded tray of fresh patisseries. Before offering one to Alex and pouring himself a coffee, he smiled and kissed her on each cheek.

'When Luc decided to create a museum Gertrud was available,' Elspeth said. 'Her father was a Swiss banker, a school friend of Luc's.'

'Her papa wasn't a banker then, of course,' Philippe interjected mildly, with a sly wink at Alex. Still a good-looking man in his mid-fifties, the lines engraved on his face indicated strength but, more importantly, the good humour which had led Elspeth to settle so happily with him.

His wife rapped his knuckles with a large wooden spoon. While they talked, she had excused herself, saying she must prepare the evening meal as their chef was taking a break.

'Although it's off-season, we've several guests. Luckily, casual tourists tend to reach us before they spot the Coq d'Or.'

Alex knew of their main rival — a larger hotel farther along the main street — and had met its owner, Auguste Jalabert. She hadn't liked him, without being able to say why.

Elspeth stirred a cauldron of soup, enough to feed the town of Sarlat.

'As I was saying — ' she reverted to the subject of the museum, ignoring her husband — 'Gertrud set the ball rolling, but now that St Justin plans a festival, the chateau needs a lively, professional eye, someone who will make its history — and what a heart-breaking history — come to life.'

'Well,' Alex said cautiously, because the wooden spoon was still weaving dangerous pirouettes in. the air, 'I'd like to set up a picture history of the entire village and, as an extra lure, create as a chateau centrepiece the story of Marcel,

Celestine and the necklace.'

'The tunnel from the keep, down to their grotto, is an extra attraction, of course. It was meant as an escape route if the fortress was ever besieged,' Elspeth reminded her. 'Those were turbulent days. In time the tunnel was forgotten. And perhaps Marcel was happy for it to be so. He never married, so rumours of a wealthy bride were wrong.'

'How wonderfully romantic,' sighed Alex. 'Why was I born too late, why did I miss out on troubadours and the Courts of Love?'

'You did well to avoid Casanova,' suggested Philippe with a smile.

'Perhaps you're right. I would have been a pushover!'

★   ★   ★

Later, as she slid into the strappy silk top and short pyjamas she wore for bed, smiling again at the way they'd joked about the old-age art of love, she wondered how, if, or when it might come into her own life. Temptation nibbled at the edge of her mind. Scrabbling in her bag, her fingers closed around the scrap of paper which bore the Giravels' phone number. Did she dare use it?

Raoul must have known, even romanced other women since his wife's death. Surely he was too masculine for it to be otherwise!

What had she been like, his dead wife, the woman who'd known his passion? Pretty special if, even ten years later, he'd never remarried.

Berating herself for foolish fancies, her thoughts lingered on the dark, enigmatic man with whom she'd shared that one brief moment of recognition. She had fired a challenge and instantly he'd responded.

Her lips compressed, recognising the stony truth. If she showed herself willing, he might wine and dine her a few times. He'd make glorious love to her. And then he'd spit her out.

A schoolgirl fantasy, that's all it is!

Screwing up the note, she flung it into the wastepaper basket, and went to bed.

4

A few days later, when Luc and Jenna arrived from Paris, Alex had spent many hours working out a possible blueprint for the exhibition.

Hopefully, with the genuine Oriental necklace also on show, her plans would attract extra visitors for St Justin's Week. Madame Dupont said the main events would take place in the promenade between the river and the main street.

'They will barricade the road for a few hours each day, and the shops should do good trade. People who come will be eating and drinking, as well as spending their money on stalls and sideshows.'

Alex didn't doubt those sharp eyes and ears, nor the housekeeper's ability to earn a living as a newshound! Final decisions about the festival would be made at a meeting of local traders, which she and Luc would attend. At the last minute, Jenna had decided not to join them.

'I'm fine,' she insisted. 'But it's been a busy day and Michel's brother or sister is kicking disapproval.' She brushed aside Luc's concern. 'Darling, don't fuss! If it makes you feel easier, you can put Michel to bed before you leave. Madame Dupont will feed me. I shan't starve.' Cupping a hand around her mouth she rolled her eyes in the direction of the kitchen. 'But I might be killed with kindness!'

'To say nothing of being talked to death,' grinned Luc.

They made an attractive couple, thought Alex, Luc with his cropped dark hair and strong features, Jenna with silver-grey eyes and long fair hair caught in her habitual ponytail. For formal dinners in Paris with Luc, she wore it swept behind her ears and held in a jewelled clasp, but confessed that she loved coming to St Justin 'so I can let my hair down!'

★   ★   ★

Meetings of the local council and traders were held in the function room of the Auberge des Fleurs. The custom originated in the days when Philippe's father had been chairman of the council, and continued after his death.

'Tradition is very important here,' explained Luc as he and Alex walked down from the chateau. 'Graves in the churchyard bear testament to families who have lived here for generations. Much of the employment is seasonal, of course, so the younger folk have to travel daily to Sarlat, or perhaps Bergerac and other towns, but can. still live at home. It's good that many of them are happy keeping to the old ways.' His smile was rueful. 'There are exceptions, of course, and you'll probably meet at least one tonight.'

Alex liked Jenna's husband. He bore an uncanny resemblance to the portrait of his father, the late count, an imposing reminder of his aristocratic heritage. One of the few remaining paintings, it hung above the fireplace in the great hall. The same firm jaw indicated a man who wouldn't tolerate fools lightly, but the curve of his mouth indicated humour and compassion.

His concern for Jenna was plain as he told Alex that this second pregnancy was less straightforward than the first.

'I'm so relieved you're willing to help us,' he said as they reached the arched doorway of the inn. 'Jenna would have tried to do far too much, even without the problems Michel's brother or sister is presenting.' He smiled down at Alex. 'You have our undying gratitude.'

'Wait for results before you say any more!' Alex was laughing as they entered the Auberge des Fleurs. Philippe was waiting to usher them into the function room.

Inside, Alex found a friendly atmosphere as others arrived, all council members or local business proprietors. She sat beside a burly man who introduced himself as Jacques Cours, and told her he owned a number of canoes which he hired out for river users.

'The tourists paddle upstream, using the current to make their voyage easy. Once they reach my landing stage a few kilometres distant, they find me waiting to collect the canoes, and sometimes those who do not relish the return trip.' A deep laugh rumbled from his chest. 'Often they are wet! So it is my job to keep everyone happy and bring them safely home.' His chunky hands traced a large circle on the table.

He was easy to talk to but the man seated on Alex's right hand side was less so. In his late twenties, he told her his name was Claude Jalabert from the largest hotel in St Justin, the Coq d'Or. He was keen to stress its size and grandeur, so Alex looked suitably impressed until a shout came from the far end of the table.

'No Auguste tonight?'

Claude's inquisitor was a black-clad, twig-thin woman in her sixties. She leaned forward, thin lips pursed beneath gimlet eyes.

'That man leaves his hotel so often these days that he is quite a stranger! What mischief is he about?'

Claude merely shook his head and ignored her. But then he was forced to admit to Alex that the business belonged to his father, Auguste. He offered no reason for his parent's absence, apart from saying he would be home soon. Alex remembered meeting the man briefly during her student days, but his initially jovial manner hadn't lasted long, and she was soon dismissed as an unimportant teenager.

Alex didn't mind Claude's stringy frame, or hair the colour of straw left for too long on a stable floor, but his pale blue eyes held no warmth.

His expression was disparaging as he surveyed the large oval table where, admittedly, the chairs had to be pushed together for lack of space.

'It is time to move on,' he grumbled, not bothering to lower his voice although Elspeth was in the background serving drinks. Her lips tightened as he went on. 'This place is too small. The Coq d'Or could provide greater comfort and is famed for its hospitality.'

Fortunately Alex wasn't obliged to reply because the meeting began. Soon everyone was exchanging ideas and jotting notes as their roles during the village festival were decided.

Luc formally introduced Alex and there was unanimous approval when she suggested that the chateau could find a colourful way of illustrating the settlement's history, particularly the effect on its families when, centuries ago, their men were recruited as Crusaders. Excited and optimistic, they'd departed for the East. But what of the families they left at home?

It was agreed that each committee member would search their houses and barns for anything which could add interest to the display.

'Including old farming tools and

trailers,' said Madame Clement, a buxom widow who owned the boulangerie.

'What about your delivery van?' quipped an elderly man, winking at Alex as he began topping up her wine glass. Hastily she laid her palm across the top.

Madame Clement made a face at him with the familiarity of a long-time neighbour as everyone laughed.

It was agreed that a medieval fair should be set up beside the river, the shops and cafes along the main street decorated with flags and bunting, each offering special discounts and souvenirs. Timid fifty-something hairdresser Mademoiselle Florian gathered courage and asked, 'What about the schoolchildren? Could we ask them to sing and dance? They might love to show everyone what they know.' Seeing nods of agreement, she went on. 'They could have races and end the week with a fancy dress parade?'

A chorus of approval brought a flush

to her sallow cheeks. Each child would receive a memento of the day, it was agreed.

'And we must have fireworks on our last evening!' boomed Jacques Cours.

Business concluded, the company sat down to a superb dinner of hearty onion soup garnished with aoli and garlic croutons, followed by chicken breast with mushrooms and cream, closing with a dessert trolley that breathed of heaven. Alex noticed that Claude Jalabert didn't stint himself, although she didn't hear him offer praise. To her surprise, as the meeting ended, he helped push back her chair and extended his hand.

'It has been a pleasure to meet you, Mademoiselle Graham.'

Murmuring a noncommittal response, she gave him a slight smile and turned to join Luc. As they left the Auberge after thanking Estelle and Philippe, she was glad of the climb uphill to the chateau. Too many meals like that, plus Madame Dupont's cooking, meant that by autumn she would roll down the slope without even feeling the bumps.

Reaching home, they found Jenna comfortably lodged on a capacious settee in the salon, happy that she had completed a manuscript she'd been working on for several weeks. Despite her demanding lifestyle, any spare time was spent writing and illustrating charming storybooks for young children.

'Albert and Oswald Ant have moved into their new villa and found a canoe in the shed. They have a great adventure on the river — wearing life jackets of course!'

Then she said something which made Alex's heart jump and her fatigue vanish.

'Raoul Giravel telephoned,' she told Luc as carefully he lifted her feet, sat beside her on the brocade-covered couch, and propped her legs across his lap. 'He wants to speak to you about our empty cottage. He'd heard that it might be free, now that Pierre and

Janine Huilier have moved away. Apparently he's just purchased land in this area and needs temporary accommodation while he starts work on it.'

'Interesting!' Luc's eyebrows shot up. 'My spies suggested the Jalaberts would grab that land when Gerard Dessart died, if that's the place Raoul's bought. They must have hoped it would come on the market eventually. Dessart was almost ninety and his health had been failing for years.' Ruefully he went on, 'Stubborn old cuss with a bad temper, and point-blank refused help whenever it was offered.' Rubbing his jaw reflectively, he added 'I doubt whether his house is worth renovating, though it's old and has plenty of character. Might depend on the state of the roof, and probably the drainage too, once someone's taken a look. Could be costly. In the meantime, it's true that Raoul would need a base, somewhere close, to cut out the travel from home each day.'

Taking a chocolate from the box

which Jenna held out to him, he went on, 'He'll be working long days. That place has been neglected for years. Needs new fencing, not to mention considerable ground clearance before he could plant anything or turn it into a paying business venture.'

His hand hovered over another chocolate.

'For Auguste Jalabert its riverside location would have huge potential.' Luc's smile held a hint of satisfaction. 'Serves him right if someone else grabbed it first. He's more often away than at home these days. Doesn't pay to take your eye off the ball.' His face mirrored double satisfaction as he tasted the second chocolate. 'He was probably waiting for the price to drop. He'll be kicking himself, and probably Claude too, if they've missed it.'

'That's what I thought,' said Jenna smugly. Carefully she didn't look in Alex's direction as she leaned sideways to drop a kiss on Luc's cheek. 'Anyway, I invited Raoul to dinner tomorrow night, so that you can discuss him renting the Huilier cottage for a while. I know you've said it needs roof repairs but a few drips and damp patches won't bother Raoul, and there's no doubt it's close to the Dessart place. And,' she winked at Alex, 'We can find out from Raoul how he managed to swing one on horrid little Claude.'

'Claude is less of a problem than his father,' said Luc thoughtfully, adding again, 'Auguste Jalabert wouldn't appreciate being beaten to the finishing post. He's obviously developed business interests elsewhere these past few years, but always had a keen nose for a bargain — which Dessart's would be. I doubt it went for much.'

'Where does Auguste go gallivanting?' wondered Jenna. 'Can't be the Caribbean because there's no trace of a tan — though I daresay it'd be hidden by that great white beard of his.'

As Luc shrugged, Alex offered to make coffee. She disappeared to the kitchen while they went on to talk about recent building work on another cottage belonging to the estate. When she returned with the drinks and a plateful of tiny petits fours she found in the cupboard, Luc's eyes brightened, despite him having raided Jenna's chocolates and tucked into the meal he'd enjoyed at the Auberge des Fleurs.

Briefly they updated Jenna on decisions resulting from the meeting but soon both she and Alex were ready to go to bed.

The day had given Alex much to think about. But when she reached her room, instead of undressing, she stood at the window, staring into the night sky.

In the past, she'd enjoyed men's company but hadn't felt a burning desire to spend more than a few hours with any she knew. Raoul Giravel was different. Despite showing minimal interest in Alex, he'd imprinted his image so firmly in her mind that she hadn't been able to erase him.

The prospect of being with him for

an evening was daunting because she couldn't trust herself to hide her interest!

5

When Raoul arrived next evening, he was accompanied by his daughter. Jenna had said she'd invited the two of them, guessing that the teenager would want to see Alex again.

Lucie couldn't hide her delight and hugged Alex as an old friend. By contrast, her father's handshake was firm but brief. Alex had wondered how he'd be when they met this second time, and now she couldn't ignore the feeling that Raoul had retreated behind an even higher fence.

There was no hint that he remembered their parting in Aix, and the way he'd so slowly released her hand. Her spirits sank, even though she'd already warned herself to expect nothing.

'Good evening, Alexandrie.' His tone was courteous enough but, as she kept her own expression bright, though not too bright, she sensed the same restraint he'd previously shown. Jenna's invitation hadn't brought him even one small step closer.

Tonight he'd discarded his grey business suit, but didn't wear the jeans and casual shirt about which Alex had fantasised. Instead, his lightweight jacket of black leather was moulded to his shoulders above grey slacks, and his deep red shirt was open at the neck, revealing a strong, tanned throat. He must have brushed his dark hair but already a few unruly curls made her want to reach up and smooth them away from his brow. With a sigh, she wondered if she'd be able to sit on her hands all evening without anyone noticing, and then had to look down quickly before anyone asked what was amusing her.

Lucie had exchanged her own probable favourites, T-shirt and jeans, for a simple blue blouse and skirt, with white leather sandals.

When Alex said how nice she looked,

the girl was obviously pleased but admitted, 'Tante Marthe insisted I wore 'ladylike dress'. She is the dragon — although a very nice one,' she added hastily. 'Tante Silvie loves to have fun but even she said I mustn't wear my jeans for a dinner engagement.'

The final comment came with a droll face and peal of laughter. Then, looking at the simple navy silk shift dress that Alex was wearing with high-heeled strappy sandals, she added, 'You look lovely, Alex, but I'm sure you always do!'

Alex suspected her cheeks had taken on an extra glow, knowing Raoul had overheard, and for a fleeting second his eyes registered agreement.

Jenna had told her the two men had known each other for some years. Although moving in different circles nowadays — Luc an architect in Paris, Raoul a vintner in the sprawling lands of the Dordogne — it was clear they liked and respected each other.

'I suggest that Raoul and I disappear

for a while and talk business,' said Luc, after Madame Dupont brought in a tray of drinks, 'That will give Lucie and Alex time to catch up with each other's news.' Carrying both glasses, he led Raoul in the direction of the small study which adjoined the chateau's library.

Lucie installed herself beside Jenna who was happy to show her the latest photographs of Michel. He was an enchanting little boy, with his mother's fair hair and already traces of her artistic talent although she admitted with a laugh that she might be just a tad biased.

Earlier, while she and Alex helped Madame Dupont prepare dinner and lay the table, Luc had taken his small son to bed. The toddler would sleep until morning.

'With luck!' was Luc's wry comment as he'd tossed Michel over his shoulder and pretended to swing him like a monkey when they ascended the grand staircase. A small microphone beside the child's cot was connected to kitchen and dining room, a necessary precaution in this vast place, so his parents could relax, knowing he was safe.

By the time Luc returned from the library with Raoul, their business settled, dinner was ready.

The dining room was a place of one-time grandeur with faded tapestry curtains, and long gleaming table bearing branched candlesticks. Thanks to Jenna's seating plan, although she would have sworn innocence, Alex found herself directly opposite Raoul, with Lucie beside her. The girl clearly shared a close relationship with her father and, although she said little, her maturity meant she was at ease in tonight's company.

Madame Dupont served an aromatic cauldron of game soup with crusty rolls, after which Alex and Lucie helped carry in the main course, duck à l'orange with locally-grown mangetout and baby carrots. Lucie chattered happily, not hiding her pleasure at seeing Alex again.

As they ate, conversation predominantly concerned Raoul's purchase of the Dessart land. Alex was content to listen, glad there was no need for direct conversation with the man whose dark attraction wasn't so much in his looks but from the essence he breathed of the open spaces, a man at one with land from which generations of his family had made their living.

'Monsieur Dessart's failing health meant he'd neglected it for years,' said Raoul. 'According to the notaire I met in Aix, the old man had no funds to employ labour and refused any help neighbours offered. When he died, his lawyers disclosed that he'd stipulated the sale must be dealt with by agents in the south, property firms with no connections in St Justin. On that front he was adamant. It seems he trusted no one locally with his affairs.'

'So who inherits?' asked Luc.

'The only heir is an equally old, distant male cousin in Hungary. A bachelor with no family.'

'Who obviously had no interest in a chunk of French soil,' said Jenna as she pushed the vegetable tureen closer to Raoul.

Luc poured more red wine into his guest's goblet, and raised an enquiring eyebrow at Lucie, who smilingly indicated that she still had enough lemonade.

'Whatever his circumstances, the Hungarian took no time in putting the land up for sale.' Raoul frowned slightly. 'Presumably he had no one to come and inspect his inheritance, or they might have spotted a generous purchaser in the shape of Auguste Jalabert.'

'I wonder if that was the reason for Dessart's insistence on the sale being dealt with outside this area.' Luc swirled the contents of his own wine glass, frowning slightly. 'It's old gossip, but I remember hearing that he'd fallen out badly with Jalabert years ago.'

'Although Auguste owns the Coq

d'Or, you'll have gathered that nowadays it's his little squirt of a son, Claude, who does the day-to-day management,' Jenna elaborated, in response to Alex's look of enquiry. 'Father and Squirt could have made good use of Dessart's land and a tidy profit eventually because it reaches from their boundary, and forms a broad strip of land down to the riverbank. Great tourist potential!'

Lucie turned to Alex. 'At the bistro you must have noticed my panic when Claude passed the window. I couldn't believe he was there! It could only be for one reason.'

'Of course! That's who it was!' Alex recalled the man she'd seen in the street outside, not interested in, and seemingly of no concern, to anyone inside La Tomate. There, he'd been hurrying past, nothing but a stranger avoiding the rain showers. 'At the St Justin meeting last night I had a feeling I'd seen him before, but couldn't think where.'

'I was terrified he would be at the notaire's office, signing the papers, before Papa got there,' explained Lucie. 'It would have been disaster!'

Raoul's lean features were relaxed as he looked across the table at the girl. 'Not really disaster, but farewell to an adventure.'

'An adventure?' Alex met his eyes, although for much of the time she had carefully not looked in his direction. His presence in this friendly atmosphere was disturbing, especially since it was impossible to forget the reserve with which he'd greeted her, and the way his fingers had released hers instantly. A cold shower would feel much the same, she reckoned.

No one in the dining room, and certainly not Alex, could have guessed the turbulence raging inside Raoul. She was waiting for an answer, but all he could concentrate on were her curving lips, small straight nose, and magnificent, riotous curls through which he longed to run his fingers.

Beside the ready smile which lurked behind her eyes he knew a dimple would appear when the smile grew wider. She was enchanting! He envied Lucie the easy rapport they'd established before he arrived at the bistro in Aix. Leaving there, he'd felt an exciting, but unwelcome, fire throbbing his veins. That way led to danger! And to disillusionment.

He hadn't doubted that Lucie would want to contact her again. It should have been simple. All he needed to do was to ring and suggest a dinner date. But where would that lead? Instinct whispered that this golden girl, tanned from the desert sun, was different. He'd enjoyed discreet and brief liaisons since Melanie died. Heaven knew, he was no monk, but time spent with women had been swift, superficial, with no commitment or recriminations. Just goodbye.

That would be impossible with Alexandrie Graham. If she entered his life, would he ever be able to let her go? And yet to have her forge a place in his heart was impossible. Melanie was dead but, by heavens, she'd possessed spirit! And so did this woman. What tricks would she employ once, inevitably, that initial magic faded?

Not that Melanie's actions could be classed as tricks. No, her guile had gone deeper. Was there no end to a woman's betrayal? Surely, the lesson was engraved on his soul.

There was no danger of him succumbing to this one's wiles. And yet . . .

His thoughts returned to that first day, when the air had crackled with awareness, making him as gauche as a teenager. He could have sworn Alex felt it too. Tonight she was facing him across a candlelit table, the air was warm, conversation easy and he was consumed by desire to know her better. Madness! Impatiently he thrust a hand through his hair. What had she just said?

For heaven's sake, pull yourself together, imbecile! She asked about the Dessart land.

'We want to create a vineyard which uses new methods — new to us, at least, although they are proving successful across France.' He forced himself to speak calmly as though he'd been searching for simple, layman's terms. His gaze was direct although the light in his dark eyes was, Alex knew, nothing to do with her but with his own plans.

'My home, La Petite Grotte vineyard, was inherited from my father and, before him, my grandfather. They cultivated it for years. It has always been quite difficult to work because the land consists mainly of terraces cut along the limestone cliffs. Our harvests can be good but the steep, narrow access is hard to farm.' He frowned briefly, as though he was visualising long hours spent toiling there.

'These new Dessart hectares are on flat terrain with gentle slopes towards the river, and will be much easier to manage. Also,' the corner of his mouth tilted slightly, 'I'm keen to try my luck with a system which can yield good results, but one where I need advice and,' at last he smiled, 'optimism.'

'And the system is what?' asked Alex, fascinated by the enthusiasm that made him lean forward, eyes alight.

'Biodynamic wine-growing.' His hand sketched an imaginary circle in the air. 'One works in time and tune with the elements, the soil, the phases of the moon.'

'I've read a little about it,' said Alex, wrinkling her forehead. 'It truly does revert to nature.'

'That's right!' added Jenna. 'It sounds a bit weird but you fill cow horns with manure and then bury them down by the roots. When the time is right, you dig the horns up, mix the manure with rainwater and then spray the vines with it. Every step, from planting, through to harvest, is done to a strict but natural routine.'

Even Luc looked at her in surprise until; smugly, she admitted to researching it for her publisher.

'Victoire wondered if, as a break from children's books, I'd care to do a few illustrations for a wine catalogue. Quite a light-hearted thing, not meant for a connoisseur! I said I'd try to fit it in. Sounds fascinating.'

'It's an intriguing way of making wine — harnessing your land and everything it produces, according to the tides of nature,' said Alex thoughtfully. 'And there must be at least some financial benefit for vignerons when it comes to buying fertiliser and so on. Bound to be popular nowadays, with so much concern about environmental issues.' Caught up in her own thoughts, she looked across the table at Raoul. 'But you must need quite a labour force, surely?'

He nodded, recognising her genuine interest.

'My main problem will be working two separate estates at once, of course, but for day-to-day management of La Petite Grotte I'm fortunate in having a good man who has worked with us for years. That will leave me time to concentrate on this new project.'

When they had finished eating and moved to the comfortable lounge for coffee, talk moved to the summer's celebrations in St Justin. Luc described his and Jenna's relief that Alex would be here to promote the chateau as a focal point.

'You can see how much this building,' he nodded towards the ceiling carvings and faded wallpaper, 'needs a cash injection, let alone the rest of the estate, and the village as a whole. It's a great opportunity but we need plenty in the way of interest and entertainment if we're to attract support across the region, as well as tourists. We'll work on publicity angles — posters, newspapers, local television and radio of course.'

Raoul had turned to face her directly. His long legs were crossed and, for the first time, he appeared relaxed as he spoke to her.

'Your interest in history and your work in the East will be valuable, but what have you in mind for an exhibition?'

Alex found no difficulty in running through the list of ideas she had talked over with Luc, and steps they had taken to acquire tapestries, military regalia and colourful standards to brighten the great hall.

'Celestine's wonderful necklace will occupy a central position, of course,' she said, her eyes sparkling as imagination once more took hold. 'We'll install tiny spotlights in the showcase to show it off to advantage.'

'And have an armed guide at each corner, ready to warn off anyone who gets too close,' chimed in Jenna. 'Shouldn't really be necessary because Alex plans to sit beside it every night with a loaded shotgun!'

Raoul's face broke into the first complete smile that Alex had seen, and his laugh rang out. White teeth, eyes lit with amusement, he looked her up and down, assessing her slender body, in much the way that he had in Aix. This time, however, she didn't feel that sense of outrage. This time she felt — how did she feel? To her chagrin, she realised what she felt was sheer joy that at last he'd cracked the wall of steel around his natural self and shared a moment of laughter with her.

Lucie had been sitting quietly, clearly enjoying the evening. Now, with diffidence, she spoke up.

'Alex, you said that, during St Justin's Week, you want the chateau to show medieval life in a way that is real. Would it be of interest to have people working on local crafts, say woodwork, silverwork jewellery or,' her face eager, 'perhaps Papa would let me bring my loom and work one of my tapestries? I could wear the costume a girl would have worn in those days.' She turned first to Raoul and then to Alex. 'Tante Silvie spends hours weaving wonderful pictures on her frame, with wools or silks, and says I am growing quite expert.' She gave a self-deprecating laugh but there was no mistaking the plea in her eyes.

'That sounds a fantastic idea!' said Alex, already visualising the busy scene within the great hall. 'Craftwork, especially St Justin 'specialities', would bring real-life atmosphere to the main rooms. But,' she cast a glance at Raoul, 'we'd need to ask your father's permission, of course.'

'It would be the school holidays,' Lucie reminded him. Her expression clouded as he stayed silent. 'The only nuisance to you would be bringing me and collecting me.' Then, cautiously, 'I could stay with you in the Huilier cottage, Papa, which would be quite close to the chateau.'

'Always assuming the two of us can manage to feed and clothe ourselves there, and I must start work quickly if we're to have a new vineyard,' came the cautionary note from her father.

'My Aunt Silvie could come with us,' said Lucie impulsively. Clapping her hands, she broke into laughter. 'She'd love it! You know she would!'

Jenna carefully avoided Alex's eyes.

'It sounds a splendid idea! And to have Lucie here with her tapestry as a living, breathing example of those early days would be perfect. We need all the help we can get. Do say yes, Raoul!'

Out-manoeuvred, although it was clear he'd prefer to say no, he inclined his head.

'It can be managed.' Addressing Alex and hiding any reluctance, he added, 'Perhaps we should arrange for you to visit La Petite Grotte. My father stored a great collection of farm implements and equipment in one of our old barns. Some could be of interest for your exhibition.'

As blue eyes met his black-browed gaze, they held for a moment and then he swung away, holding out his hand to Lucie.

'Come, mon enfant, it is time for us to leave.'

Kissing Jenna on each cheek as he thanked her and Luc for their hospitality, he hesitated in front of Alex, before

101

inclining his head in a slight bow. 'We shall meet again quite soon.'

And then they were gone.

6

A few days later, Alex strolled along the pathway beside the village shops and cafes, glancing occasionally across the wide promenade to where a few small boats were tucked alongside the river bank.

A handful of holidaymakers and some locals exchanged casual greetings as they enjoyed their aperitif or coffee in the sunshine, and a plump hand waved to her from the window of the boulangerie.

Soon she found herself outside the Coq d'Or hotel. More imposing than the Auberge des Fleurs, and attractive in a more upmarket way, its stone façade and miniature turrets were softened by windowboxes which in summer probably spilled over with geraniums but now were bright with spring flowers. From there onwards, a few small houses straggled to show this was the end of the village and, beyond them, she could see the land which Raoul now owned. Instantly she realised what an advantage it could be to the Jalaberts. It would have extended their grounds to the very edge of the water.

A short, tubby man came down the hotel steps as she passed the front entrance. A few paces behind him came Claude Jalabert.

'Mademoiselle Graham!' the younger man called, recognising Alex.

Cursing silently, Alex stopped and summoned a smile.

'Alex, please!'

As the men reached the pavement, Claude took her hand in a limp greeting.

'I would like you to meet my father. I told him how you plan to make a great success of the chateau's summer festival.'

The older man's grip was strong as it closed on her slim fingers.

'Enchanté, Mademoiselle Alex! I am delighted to meet you. I am Auguste Jalabert. Claude told me the results of the meeting. Unfortunately I was away on business, or I would have enjoyed putting in a few ideas of my own!'

Alex didn't doubt that he'd have plenty to say. Instinctively she didn't like him. His pale blue eyes were too hard, his handshake as determined as a gorilla that wanted to crush her. It was impossible to refuse his invitation to go into the hotel for what he described as 'a small aperitif'.

The interior breathed tasteful comfort, its decor and furnishings in keeping with the style of 'old' France, and not a hint of glass or chrome-topped table in sight. She had no doubt that the menu she spotted, a vellum-style scroll at the entrance to an elegantly-appointed dining room, offered and delivered excellent food. It was impressive but she still preferred the smaller, family-style atmosphere of the Auberge des Fleurs where even now, she suspected, Elspeth and Philippe would be readying themselves for the evening's business.

In a smaller, equally finely-furnished room, he closed and locked a door leading to what Alex assumed was his private office, tucking the key into an inner pocket of his jacket. With a smile, he indicated a comfortable chair beside the window.

'Did you have a successful trip?' she enquired, sitting as he proffered a delicate glass of what he described as 'something special from my travels'. Tasting it gingerly, she smiled at him. 'This is delicious!'

He looked pleased. He could have been a garden gnome in some other life, she decided with an inward chuckle. *If ever I built a rockery, I'd stick him there, in a cheery red coat and green trousers. Or would he make a better Santa Claus?* She shook away her fantasies and realised he was asking about her work. Claude must have passed on the information he'd gleaned from the St Justin meeting.

'I understand you are an archaeologist. Such a wonderful, absorbing career.' Clearly he'd forgotten their first encounter years ago, when he'd dismissed a teenager as being of no account, but she decided not to remind him.

His interest seemed genuine and his knowledge of current and past excavations, in Europe and the wider world, surprisingly extensive. When Alex said as much, he admitted that ancient history had been his passion since his schooldays. 'Now that Claude can conduct much of my hotel's business, I am free to indulge my hobby.'

He drew Alex out to talk about her digs in the East, and sympathised with the problems of working far from home.

'I'm considering an excavation in northern England where there may be interesting domestic finds,' she admitted. 'My mother would be glad to have me back in Europe, at least for a while.'

Jalabert said he had spent a few weeks in Northumberland, visiting various Roman settlements, so time passed swiftly as they talked about extraordinary finds along the ancient wall.

'Who knows what else is hidden there?' His eyes dropped to her small, capable hands. 'And you might scrape away the soil that hides them!'

Eventually, glancing at the heavy antique pendulum clock, she began to rise but he put out his hand to delay her.

'In my travels I have viewed some wonderful private archives, and certain items have been worth a fortune.' Stroking his beard, he leaned closer until she felt his warm breath on her cheek. 'There must be moments when you discover a muddy object and think *This isn't of value in itself* — a *pottery jug, or battered tunic-clasp.* But you realise how an avid collector would cherish it.'

Alex heard him with the first tingles of a growing unease as he went on, 'I have met decent men who would collect and cherish such a piece. They suspect that too often, its fate will be a cardboard box tucked away on some museum shelf.' Taking her hand, he squeezed it slightly in a fatherly way. 'And now I must not keep you. But remember — I have many contacts who take interest in the ancient world.' He tapped the side of his nose with a stubby forefinger and once more stroked his beard. 'The day may come when you need a little financial help and a friend.'

Alex disentangled her hand and managed a slight laugh.

'I know you're joking, of course, but I suspect you're right about there being plenty of — ' she wanted to say *unscrupulous criminal sharks* — 'private collectors out there!'

Ugh! Alex somehow managed to thank him pleasantly for his hospitality and the chance to take a look inside his hotel. Standing outside the iron-studded door, he raised his hand in farewell as, abandoning her earlier plans, she walked back towards the terrace steps to the chateau.

He'd been sounding her out! He'd made sure she knew he was in the market, presumably a collectors' agent, for ancient valuables. There was a huge black market dealing in them and he'd given her an open invitation. What a slug! Again, she shuddered.

A voice from behind made her turn. Claude! Oh no, she could do without any more of the Jalaberts today. But he began walking beside her.

'I wonder if you would care to drive out of the village one evening, and have dinner with me? I know one or two pleasant restaurants and would like to spend some time with you.'

Quickly she seized on the one word that offered a let-out, and he just might believe it.

'Time! Oh Claude, you've said the magic word! With the exhibition and festival galloping at full speed toward me, I daren't take even one evening off. But thank you very much for your invitation.'

He looked less than pleased but managed a slight laugh. 'I shall ask you again, but not until your duties permit. Be sure to let me know before the time comes when you must leave us!'

With a nod and slight wave, he left her. Alex let out a long sigh of relief.

As she reached home, she met Madame Dupont who was carrying a basket of salad stuff which, she explained, came from one of the cottage gardens long abandoned on the lower terrace.

'Every piece of good soil is used here, whether or not the building is in ruins. I saw young Albert from the boulangerie working on his plot and he gave me these.' As Alex took the basket from her and they went towards the kitchen, she added quietly, 'We saw you leaving the Coq d'Or.'

The housekeeper didn't notice Alex's

amusement. No need for a town crier or local journal when Madame Dupont was around! Admitting to her aperitif and chat with Auguste Jalabert, she wasn't surprised when the other woman scowled. It was obvious that she neither liked nor trusted the man.

'As for Claude, they say there was a great quarrel with his father recently.' Starting to pack away lettuce and, radishes from the basket, she added that Claude had a penchant for gambling. 'Maybe he prefers the races or the card table to a day's honest work. That would be like a flame to a rocket where his father is concerned!'

Opening the refrigerator, she took out meat intended for dinner, and carried on talking.

'I heard it said that Auguste wanted to buy the Dessart land but Claude had visited the races and reached the notaire's office too late. They say Auguste had money to develop the riverbank, even build a cafeteria, ice-cream stall and so on. It could have made him rich.'

'He seems pretty rich already,' said Alex, remembering the understated affluence within the Coq d'Or, and the cost of Auguste's travels, which he'd freely described, covering nearly every corner of the globe.

Madame Dupont nodded sagely.

'He would have a finger in every pie possible, that one. When we were all at school he was known for his cheating ways!'

7

During the following days, Alex's plans for the chateau exhibition took shape, as did the festival committee's plans for the village.

She had attended several more meetings but, to her relief, there was no sign of Claude Jalabert and it seemed that his father was once again travelling. From the schoolrooms to the boulangerie, the pavement cafes and scaffolding being erected along the river bank, she loved the knowledge that everyone around her was involved, and keen to do what they could to make St Justin Week a success.

Jenna and Luc had returned home to Paris so she was reliant on Madame Dupont for local news, including the fact that Raoul Giravel was widely regarded as the perfect man to bring the Dessart vineyard to life once more.

His father had done the same years ago with the terraces of La Petite Grotte, a few kilometres distant. Raoul hadn't yet moved into the Huilier cottage and wasn't likely to be around, so Alex, curious, drove the short distance to the old Dessart homestead one afternoon, telling herself it was natural neighbourly interest.

Rusting wrought-iron gates were open as she reached the estate, so she drove slowly along the winding dirt-track for more than two hundred metres before sighting any buildings. Stretching on either side were acres of land that, even to a novice like herself, looked in need of care. Rows of gnarled vine roots were budding in the warm spring sunshine, but would soon be choked by swathes of creeper and long tongues of persistent shrub which crept along the dry earth.

The potential of this place was huge, Alex realised, as her eyes scanned sweeping reaches which sloped towards the river, hardly a kilometre distant. It was small wonder Raoul had been anxious to buy this! One day, hard work and the passage of time would make it a wonderful vineyard. A place that he could call his own, with no ties to the past.

The old farmhouse came into sight, its mellow golden stones reflecting sunlight which streamed across a central, weed-choked courtyard. Rough grasses spiking among tall white daisies and sprawling shrubs told the story of a once-loved garden, now abandoned to nature.

What she hadn't bargained for, as she drew up outside the low, sprawling building, was to see Raoul himself, busy repairing another dilapidated gate which led to the house and stone barns.

Dismayed, she waved an airy greeting and was about to accelerate away when he put up an arm to slow her down. As she drew her blue run-about to a halt, he came closer, his eyes amused they scanned the dusty vehicle.

'I would expect nothing more than a motorised toy from a woman who enjoys grubbing around in Egyptian dust,' he remarked coolly. He pulled open the driver's door. 'You have decided to take a look. So come and satisfy your curiosity!'

Embarrassment at being found spying was quickly forgotten. Alex retorted, 'Someone should have taught you some manners!'

A shadow passed across his face.

'Unfortunately, unlike you, I had no mother to teach me any!'

Disconcerted, she bit her lip and then, low-voiced, said, 'I'm sorry. I didn't realise you lost her when you were so young.'

He shrugged. 'It is of no importance. She was without maternal feeling.'

'What do you mean?'

Again he shrugged as they walked towards the door of the house.

'Her roots were far south, in the Camargue. And that is where she fled.'

'You mean, it isn't that she died? It's that she left you here?'

Inclining his dark head, he growled, 'With my father, who had a vineyard to work, and a child to bring up. There was little time to teach manners in the beginning. And then, years later, the pattern was repeated!'

She could tell from the sudden way his lips compressed that he regretted saying so much and yet, to her, it seemed as though a cauldron of feeling was there, waiting for release.

It wasn't like Alex to hold back from asking what he meant but they were inside the house and he began describing the renovation work needed. The previous conversation had ended.

'Fortunately, the structure is good and strong, but the roof needs replacing. Then I can be rid of the damp. Kitchen and bathroom need replacing too, and I want to install at least one shower.'

Although the downstairs rooms were drab and musty, their windows smeared and cobwebby, two had big fireplaces with wood-burning stoves which must at one time have sent comforting warmth throughout the house. Upstairs, Alex counted four bedrooms, and space where Raoul could build the showers he envisaged.

'It could be lovely,' she said, looking around and imagining the charming home it would become. 'It will take time, but you'll not be beaten!'

His rare smile lit his face as he bowed mockingly.

'Merci, mademoiselle, for your kind encouragement!'

Expecting sarcasm, she was taken aback by his obvious pleasure. Was praise so rare for him? There must be someone other than Lucie in his life, someone who took an interest in what he did? Risking a snub, she asked a little diffidently, 'Is there a chance that Lucie's aunts and their families will help with some of the donkey work?'

Surprise made him throw back his dark head and laugh out loud.

'Lucie's aunts? Marthe and Silvie between them number about a hundred and fifty years. They would be willing, but I could not send them climbing ladders and wielding paintbrushes!' And then, seeing Alex's bewilderment, he explained that the two women were his father's sisters, living together. 'Until I lost my mother. Now they care also for Lucie.'

Alex didn't dare speak but then, as the silence grew, felt she must ask more.

'Lucie told me she was very young when her mother died. I'm so sorry.' Sympathy warmed her voice and she was completely unprepared for his violent reaction.

His arm swept the air, narrowly missing a battered oil lamp which must have been a back-up for Dessart when the electricity supply failed.

'Save your sympathy, for God's sake! I have no need of it. We do better without her!'

Aghast, she wondered what morass she'd blundered into.

'She was American. She died in

America.' He swung open the front door, clearly closing the subject and eager for Alex to leave.

But then, calming, and probably reading her dismay, he spoke more quietly. There was a strange note, a mixture of welcome and reluctance, in his voice as he continued.

'You may like to visit our home at La Petite Grotte. I will speak to Marthe and Silvie. They will be happy to meet you.' His lips twisted as he added, 'And Lucie will be utterly delighted!'

8

It was Lucie who issued the formal invitation. She rang Alex early the following morning, and they arranged the visit for a few days later.

'We can ride or walk around the vineyard when you arrive, and then my aunts are looking forward to making lunch and their wonderful patisseries for you,' she said brightly. 'Our visitors are usually delivery men, or people who come to talk business, and they are no fun at all!'

She went on to suggest a lazy afternoon in Aunt Silvie's workshop, where her aunt spent hours working tapestries, and giggled when Alex confessed that she hadn't realised Marthe and Silvie were, in fact, great-aunts.

'But of course! Who else would make me wear a skirt and sensible shoes for dinner at the chateau!'

No wonder Lucie, despite her youth, had that air of maturity, even a slightly old-fashioned turn of phrase and manner. Surely she had cousins her own age, with parents a generation younger than Marthe and Silvie?

But no — Lucie, as if to make the situation clear, was saying that Raoul had no siblings. A tinge of hesitation crept into her voice as she added that her mother might have belonged to a larger family. 'But they would be in America, of course, so I do not know them.'

Alex's forehead creased a little after the call ended. Odder and odder. Surely any American relatives, despite distance, would have wanted to keep in touch with Melanie's only child? Had Raoul frozen them out?

It wasn't hard to imagine. Scarcely hidden beneath a disturbingly attractive man, one who could charm a woman until her knees gave way, there lurked a steely wall that might well prove impregnable.

Medieval Sarlat was midway between St Justin and La Petite Grotte so, two days later, Alex stopped there to buy flowers and perhaps chocolates before heading to her lunch at the vineyard. She was allowing extra time because Madame Dupont needed a rubber hose for the washing machine which had started leaking. When Alex suggested ringing a plumber, the older woman's sparse eyebrows shot up.

'Do you think I shall let such a tiny problem beat me?' she demanded. 'Why should I lavish a fortune on someone who takes his time, expects a flow of coffee, and then gives me a huge bill?'

She had described where to find the hardware store, which was tucked away in one of the narrow streets close to the centre of Sarlat, so Alex made that her first errand before buying any gifts for Lucie's great-aunts.

Wherever she'd travelled, the hidden lanes and alleyways of any city were places she loved to explore and in an ancient town like Sarlat it was easy to spend hours doing that.

As she left the hardware shop, mission accomplished, she was surprised to see Claude Jalabert sitting outside a shaded tabac/bar, drinking with two men.

This wasn't a location she'd expect the dapper, fastidious Claude to frequent, and his obvious ease in their company was also unexpected. There was no reason against him talking to a pair of workmen but, heads close together, they gave the impression of plotting mischief. So what was the son of a classy hotel owner doing with them?

Curious, she dawdled for an instant, pretending difficulty with the coil of hose as she pushed it deeper into a too-small bag. The meeting was breaking up and they shoved back their chairs, one stubbing out a cigarette, his companion, an older man, standing to slurp the final dregs of his glass. Her next surprise came when Claude, catching sight of her, hurriedly ducked his head. It was obvious he didn't want to be seen.

'Bonjour, Monsieur Jalabert!' she called jauntily, and waved a hand. That'd teach him!

Her cheery greeting forced him to lift a hand in response but it was patently clear that he hadn't wanted to be recognised. She went on her way, laughing a little, but wondering what he was up to. A seemingly furtive back-street meeting was a far cry from the superior persona he usually tried to present. Remembering hints about his gambling addiction, she realised this dingy street might be where he did his betting.

*　*　*

Armed with fragrant lilies and a box of hand-made chocolates, she was greeted warmly as she arrived at her destination. Lucie had obviously been

126

watching out for her and was beside the car, even before Alex opened the door.

Behind the teenager came her two great-aunts. Alex didn't know quite what she'd expected but the reality was a relief and a pleasure. A relief because their lively smiles and quick movements made it clear that they were far from the tottering ancients she'd anticipated. A pleasure, too, because of their beams of welcome.

Marthe was quite tall and thin, her white hair drawn back in a tight bun that reminded Alex of a particularly grim headmistress she'd once suffered. There the likeness ended because, any similar lines in the Frenchwoman's face were softened by smiley wrinkles around her eyes.

Silvie was tiny, slim, birdlike in movement. Her silvery grey hair was bobbed just below her ears and drawn back with a pale blue bandeau, the same blue as the bright eyes which were looking at the newcomer with unconcealed interest. Alex immediately felt drawn to the little woman.

She couldn't help a pang of disappointment that another figure hadn't appeared. But Raoul was sure to be working somewhere in the vineyard, either here or his new acquisition at St Justin. He'd hardly be likely to waste even minutes of his morning waiting to say *Hello, lovely to see you, how about dinner with me tomorrow night?*

After coffee and petits-fours biscuits in a comfortable if old-fashioned drawing room, Lucie was eager to take Alex outside and show her the big barns and cellars where the work of fermenting and storing wine took place.

'And then, if you can ride a horse, I have some new jeans which are too big for me, and you might enjoy travelling around on four legs, rather than your own two!'

When Alex agreed that would be lovely, Lucie eyed her trim figure and, laughing, said, 'But you are so slender, even my clothes might be too big!'

'I quite agree!' A voice came from the doorway, causing Alex's pulses to ricochet wildly. It obviously surprised Lucie as well.

'Papa! What are you doing here? I thought you were working on the far terrace today.'

'And so I shall be, but first perhaps you will let me help you show Alex our winemaking empire!' He reached out a hand and gently tugged his daughter's long hair. 'I doubt you are to be trusted when it comes to her sampling the new vintage. We don't want to be picking her up off the floor!'

Seeing him like this, relaxed and so at ease, even with her there, Alex was struck by how different he could be from the man she had first met at the bistro in Aix.

For Raoul, the sight of this golden girl, here in his own home, brought a lightness to his veins, something he knew he should ignore. Since early morning he'd told himself to keep

129

away, but as the hours passed and he knew she was there, within reach, he'd finally given in to temptation. Just to look at her, to talk to her, to see the way her deep blue eyes lit when she smiled, and beside her mouth the kissable, enticing dimple . . .

Inside a great cellar he described how, after picking and crushing the grapes, eventually the juice would ferment in large vats. 'We store it for a year, two, often more, in barrels. In here,' he said, leading her outside and into another dark and cavernous cellar cut into the limestone cliffs that reared behind the house.

Alex had been struck dumb, registering her quickened heartbeats and at the same time scolding herself for them. Managing to find her voice at last, she asked why the vineyard was called La Petite Grotte.

Raoul looked down at her, as though he'd already wondered about her unusual silence. His voice was gentle as he explained it came from a number of tiny caverns tucked away in the escarpment.

'Perhaps now you would like to taste some wine, one that makes us particularly proud.' He drew a small sample from one of a line of barrels resting on their sides, and handed it to Alex, watching with a smile as she lifted the glass, sniffed and cautiously sipped.

'Mmm!' She tilted her head, not realising the provocation of her lips, moist with red wine as, eyes half-closed, she considered her verdict. 'Deep, warm blackberry, with just a hint of lemon and rosemary.'

His black brows shot up. 'That is remarkably good! You clearly have a refined palate!'

'Are you humouring me?' she demanded.

'Would I dare?'

Lucie, as she had in Aix, was watching and listening to this by-play. Obviously loving the sight of her father at ease with Alex, she asked if he could take them around the vineyard in his estate vehicle. 'We had thought of riding, but this would save Alex from having to change her clothes, and perhaps needing safety pins to tighten the waist of my jeans!'

★ ★ ★

The following hour was one Alex felt she would remember all her life. Sunshine, blue sky, a happy teenager and a man with whom she admitted she had fallen irrevocably in love.

The vine-clad terraces must be hard work to manage and maintain, and when she said as much to Raoul, he agreed. Lean brown hands resting on the steering wheel, dark curls lifting as they drove slowly in the slight spring breeze, he reminded her of their talk over dinner at the chateau with Luc and Jenna.

'It has taken years to recover from a financial shortfall here,' he said, without enlarging on the reason. 'But recovery coincided with the time of Dessart's death. I wanted a new challenge so when his land came on the market and with it the chance to try biodynamic farming, I was desperate to reach the agent before anyone else.'

'And now you will have to watch the calendar carefully,' said Alex. 'Because you must prepare the soil, plant new vines, give the old ones some tender, loving care, and harvest in accordance with the waxing and waning of the moon.' She'd started reading about this renewal of ancient peasant culture, teamed with some modern-day methods. Bright-eyed, she looked up at him. 'Did I get that lesson right?'

Raoul's long finger played with a tendril of her curly hair, gleaming richly in the sunlight.

'Yes.' His voice was husky. 'You got it exactly!'

The silence was broken by Lucie, who had been encouraging a spider out of the vehicle.

'We have to be at lunch for twelve o'clock,' she announced. 'Can you stay and eat with us, Papa?'

'Unfortunately, no. I have to make arrangements to interview new labourers for the Dessart vineyard. Time is of the essence, as they say in England, and it's vital that there's no delay. The moon won't wait for us!'

His farewell to Alex was brief but she knew that an intangible cord was drawing them closer. One day soon, perhaps he'd ring and suggest they spend the evening together . . . She frowned. There was still something holding him back, some sort of barrier that was unnatural in such a virile, full-blooded man. What could it be?

* * *

Aunt Silvie's workroom was a revelation. A large upstairs room contained her loom and a vast array of tapestries, large and small, which she had woven over the course of many years. She was delighted to show them to Alex and explain how she'd created each scene,

134

and the story behind many of them.

'It is a longtime since we enjoyed a visit from a young woman, especially one so interested in my work,' she said. 'Marthe and I have friends, but they are growing older and less inclined to travel even the short distance from one homestead to the next. My sister has her own car but time passes swiftly and we tend to use it for shopping.'

Alex made no comment but was sad for Lucie who, it seemed, had little or no company of her own age at home. She moved the conversation to talk of the St Justin festival and exhibition.

Silvie was as excited as Lucie, accepting that the girl would want to spend much of her school holiday there, as part of the unofficial work-force. It had been agreed that, wearing medieval costume, the teenager would work on a loom and also a frame so that visitors could watch how the different tapestries came into being. Proud of her great-niece's skill, Silvie assured Alex that Lucie wouldn't disappoint her.

Marthe, downstairs, had called Lucie to help in the kitchen. Reluctant to leave the workroom, Alex wandered to where a stack of small, finished examples were propped in a corner, just beyond the shelves on which Silvie stored a colourful tumble of silks and wools. One of the tapestries had fallen sideways and wasn't a landscape scene as many others, but seemed to be a portrait, with only forehead and eyes showing. Alex bent to straighten it back in the pile but suddenly halted. A woman's face looked from the canvas. Her features and smooth chestnut-brown hair were beautifully executed, a work of skilled hands and infinite patience from the talented artist who had woven it, whether from a photograph or flesh and blood original. Instantly, Alex knew who it must be, and could almost smell the musky perfume.

Silvie's wrinkled hand flew to her mouth as, with a gasp of dismay, she cast harassed eyes at the half-open door.

'Oh my goodness! This should not be

here! Oh, what have I done? What will Marthe say?' Almost snatching the tapestry from Alex, she tucked it at the back of the pile and there was little doubt that, once alone in the room again, she would hide it more effectively. Agitated fingers, ostensibly tucking stray silver wisps of hair into the blue bandeau, dislodged even more.

'There's no harm done,' said Alex, wondering at the little woman's distress. Already she realised that, by finding this image of Melanie, the young mother who died years ago, she'd stepped into forbidden territory. There was something dark here. Something connected with Raoul and Lucie. She'd not rest until she'd found out more.

Innocently she asked, 'Who is she? It's a most striking face.'

Silvie pushed the door closed. And then she whispered 'It is Melanie, Lucie's mother.' Her face twisted in a strange mixture of disgust and dislike. 'I should have burned it long ago. But Raoul destroyed all the photographs of her and I felt that perhaps one day Lucie might become curious to see her face, and should have some small reminder. The woman was, after all, the one who gave birth to her!'

Alex didn't know what to say. Lucie's great-aunt had suddenly opened a book which Raoul had forced shut. The only way to find out more was to ask, though it seemed uncomfortably like prying.

'I understand Melanie died when Lucie was young. Was she ill for long? Or perhaps she had an accident?'

'It was an accident. But it was in America. She was with another man.' Suddenly the little woman's eyes were wet as, unconsciously, she wrung her hands. 'We never speak of it. I have never shared this burden — and to keep such a secret is a burden!' Touching Alex's hand, she went on, 'I have only known you a few hours but already I know you care about us. From the day of meeting Lucie, you and she have shared a great rapport. She loves you, and knows we have found a friend. You will keep our secret.' Before Alex could ask, she added, 'She saw the tapestry one day and knew it was her mother.'

'Another man!' This was the last thing Alex had imagined. How could any woman have left a husband like Raoul?

Drawing a deep breath, she took the thin hand in hers. It was as though the sight of Melanie's face, hidden behind a pile of dusty needlework, had unlocked in Silvie a haunting need to tell a truth that had been forbidden talk for years.

'She was in the man's car when it crashed.'

'Did he die too?'

'Thankfully, yes! May the saints forgive me for saying so!'

'What on earth do you mean?'

The door burst open and Alex was forced to quell her frustration.

★ ★ ★

The rest of the afternoon passed without incident. Over coffee and delicious gateaux made by Marthe they discussed arrangements for Lucie to be part of the chateau exhibition once school closed for the summer. Silvie seemed recovered from her distress — perhaps, wondered Alex, because she had spoken of the forbidden at last.

Endearingly, the little woman was as excited as a child at the prospect of housekeeping for her great-niece and Raoul at the Huilier cottage, while work progressed on the new vineyard. It was near enough to the chateau for Lucie to walk to her temporary 'employment' but more likely that Raoul when possible, or Alex, would act as her chauffeur.

As Alex drove away from La Petite Grotte, her mind was reeling with an entirely new vision of past events, the cataclysm which turned Raoul into the man she now knew. If he'd been deserted by his mother, and then, years later, by the wife he adored, what chance did an out-of-work archaeologist ever stand of winning his trust?

And without trust, how could there be love?

Within a few weeks it would become, even more, an impossible dream.

9

All too soon it was early summer — but Alex was ready and so was the village of St Justin.

She hadn't seen Raoul for a few weeks but knew, through Silvie, who was now established in the Huilier cottage, that he was working 'like a man possessed'.

Lucie stayed there every weekend, impatient for school to break up, when she could be there more often. She, Silvie and Alex had become good friends, drawn together by mutual love of history, needlework art, and support of Raoul in what he'd termed his 'adventure'.

By now he had his own temporary army of labourers to tackle the backlog created by old man Dessart's lack of money and workforce. Two were repairing boundary fences, another couple were clearing acres of scrubland, while around the old vines a mass of persistent bracken was being uprooted by two young hikers, who came looking for temporary work.

Raoul planned to cultivate the long-established vines alongside new plants, and hope that old and young would do well. Elsewhere, he'd employed a stonemason to make good an outbuilding where machinery could be kept dry, and the large cavern which would hold great vats and wooden barrels.

A few were already there, filled with wine from the Dessart years. In years to come, others would hold each new vintage.

The place was buzzing, thought Alex, her lips curving with pleasure as she drove Lucie and Silvie back to the Huilier cottage one afternoon. Lucie had a day off school so she, Silvie and Alex had spent a couple of happy hours at the chateau. The needlework work-shop was in reality a large, bright alcove extending from the main hall of the museum. Here, once her holidays began, Lucie would sit working a loom. On the stone walls there hung examples of tapestry for visitors to admire. Already a few early tourists had wandered around, seeming to find the museum and its exhibition interesting and worth their ticket money. When Silvie could find time to be there, some were intrigued to learn from her about the art of weaving. If they could spend an hour or more, she sent them home with a small example of their own work.

'Don't forget that I'll be away for a couple of days at the end of the week,' Alex reminded them as they climbed out of her car at the cottage. 'My mother and the rest of the family will never forgive me if I miss my cousin's wedding!'

She had forgotten about the family gathering until ten days ago when Eloise telephoned from Aix-en-Provence to ask if Alex would like her to choose, and give, a present from both of them.

'I've a copy of their wedding gift list, and thank goodness there's plenty that we can afford,' laughing. 'And plenty that we can't!'

★ ★ ★

Driving southwards the day before the wedding, Alex was looking forward to seeing so many of her friends and relations — a rare event because she'd been working away so much and contact was difficult. Everyone was busy with their lives.

Her cousin Blanche, two years younger than Alex, had been engaged to Alain, a young stockbroker since last year. Alex liked him instantly when they met on the eve of the ceremony.

It was a lovely, sunny day for the wedding, and a great opportunity for floaty chiffon dresses or elegant shot-silk sheaths to have an airing, mostly topped by fabulous hats — although some were little more than a knot of flowers trapped in a wisp of lace. Alex had treated herself, deciding it was time for an ultra-feminine fantasy completely different to the tough shorts or jeans she wore when working, either on a dig, or at the chateau. Pale green, the gently-swathed neckline of the dress outlined her slim throat and was the perfect foil for her sunshine-gold hair, held today behind her ears by an artful twist of tiny white gardenia blossoms. The skirt fell tulip-style from her waist to just below her knees and her feet were shod in cream court shoes with impossibly high heels. Eloise had viewed them with a sceptical eye, suggesting a need for sticking plasters when she fell over. Alex admitted that she'd wondered the same, but couldn't resist!

Family and friends wanted to hear about her project in St Justin, but were even more keen to know if she'd met some nice French men there, specifically one to marry and settle with, here in France. What would they say if she admitted that she'd found the man of her dreams, but all she could expect from him was a brief affaire?

Instead, laughing, Alex promised to keep her eyes open, but dashed their hopes by confessing a greater passion for deserts and buried stones. 'Although, once summer ends, I might look for an excavation nearer home,' she told them. 'But it'll have to be an exciting one.' With that they had to be satisfied, although the bride artfully threw her bouquet so that Alex was the girl to catch it.

She'd half-expected Eloise to return to St Justin with her and spend a couple of weeks there, if not more. However, her mother had more exciting plans. She had recently enjoyed dinner and several outings with a university colleague.

'He's a professor of intellectual history, so we've a lot in common,' she said. And then, rather diffidently, added 'I must admit that, although I'll never forget your father, it is rather a treat to have a man's company sometimes.'

Anxiously, 'You don't mind, do you, cherie?'

'Don't be silly — of course not! I don't want you to be lonely, and goodness knows, any man would love to have you as a friend. Or more.' Hugging her mother reassuringly, Alex added, 'I had the best father in the world, but there's no way he'd resent you getting on with your life.'

The drive from Aix northwards again was pleasant with the car hood down, her mind filled with happy memories of the wedding, the church full of relations she hadn't seen for ages, and everyone glad to see 'the wanderer', as they described her. As on her first trip to St Justin, she stopped overnight at Villeclos, but next morning left early, knowing there was plenty of work waiting for her at the chateau.

Tired of motorways and busy highways, on a whim she branched off the main road, deciding to drive through the small town of St Cloud. It would only add a couple of miles to the journey. There was less chance of traffic along this quiet country road . . . something she soon came to regret.

Less than eight miles from St Justin, and before reaching St Cloud, her car issued a series of baffled grunts and stopped. Cursing, she jumped out and, opening the bonnet, was wreathed in billows of smoke. Her rough working knowledge of mechanics was enough to confirm the worst. There was no quick-fix to this one.

Reaching inside the glove compartment, she grabbed her phone and then double-cursed. A few minutes before she'd left Aix, Eloise had reminded her to collect several boxes of antiques which one of the museums there was willing to lend for the festival. With one eye on the clock, and hurrying, Alex had forgotten to charge her mobile. The battery was as dead and unresponsive as the car. Now what?

The afternoon sun was hot and although a mile, or possibly eight, of walking wasn't a problem, she dared not leave the vehicle, even in this remote spot. The canvas hood of her car offered no security for a treasure-trove of another town's valuables.

One parcel was of particular importance, being a large and fragile etching, said to represent St Justin praying in the cave where he lived for years. She mustn't take any risks.

Oh well, all I can do is sit tight and wait. Someone will come eventually.

The someone turned out to be Mademoiselle Florian, the travelling hairdresser from St Justin, probably returning home after the latest cut and blow-dry. Recognising the little blue car, she drew up behind it and stopped.

'Oh, ma petite!' Nervously she fluttered her hands, hands that daily wielded ferocious scissors over a dozen willing heads. 'Can I help?'

Alex had got to know the hairdresser quite well during her fortnightly visits to give Madame Dupont 'a tidy' and a few titbits of the gossip she dispensed with each new hairstyle. Her sense of humour was sharp and surprisingly saucy, hidden as it was beneath her demure appearance.

She left her car and came to where Alex was sitting on the grassy bank. Her beige skirt and drab brown jacket gave no hint of the stylish hairdos she produced, but her eyes were kind.

'My radiator's given up the ghost and my 'phone's dead, so I couldn't ring for a breakdown van,' groaned Alex. Rising, she brushed a stray buttercup from her skirt. 'There's a big enough garage in St Cloud to do a repair, though perhaps not tonight.'

Mademoiselle Florian fished her own phone from a capacious pocket but, exasperated, said, 'No signal. I feared as much. It tends to be more absent than present in this area.'

Hopefully, Alex asked, 'As you go through St Cloud, could you possibly ask the garage to collect my car — and me? I'll be so grateful!'

On reaching the town — more a village really — she could hire a vehicle and re-load the precious antiques and her own belongings.

Mlle Florian offered her a lift but when Alex indicated the back seat crammed with packets, then opened the laden boot, explaining why the car couldn't be left, she understood and soon drove off, promising to call at the garage.

Almost an hour passed and Alex,. restless, bored, hungry and thirsty, was wondering when on earth salvation would arrive.

Five minutes later, she had her answer. A car stopped beside her. At the wheel sat Raoul Giravel.

10

It was hard to read the expression on Raoul's face as he slid from the dusty saloon he was driving. He wasn't wearing his customary working garb of jeans and casual denim top, but instead was clad in grey slacks and, over a white shirt, a lightweight suede jacket.

'Surely a wheelbarrow expert, such as you, can deal with a sardine-tin on wheels?' One black eyebrow raised, he'd remembered why her name was shortened to Alex, and jumped at the chance to make fun of her car.

Of all the people in the world, why did it have to be him? He would rile her, ridicule her, find numerous faults with her while she was hot, tired and longing for food and drink. And he'd set her heart pumping, her senses longing for a touch, a smile, something to show he liked her — no, more than liked her!

Gruffly, as he raised the bonnet, she snapped, 'Radiator.'

'Instant diagnosis! I congratulate you, mademoiselle!'

'If you're going to be sarcastic, please buzz off! The breakdown van will be here any minute.'

'I think not.'

'What d'you mean?'

'Only that Mlle Florian found the garage closed. The owner has gone to a funeral. I happened to be in St Cloud where I had business at the distillery, so she sent me to rescue you.' Nodding towards his car, he said 'Jump in. We can organise a garage tomorrow.'

'I can't leave the stuff I've got here. Didn't she tell you? So could you at least phone someone who isn't at a funeral?'

'My goodness! What a cross little tongue you have sometimes!' Then, seeing Alex wipe a disconsolate hand across her flushed face, he said gently in

154

his beguilingly attractive accent, 'I have a better idea, We will move all your belongings to my own vehicle, and then I will take you for something to eat while we arrange for another breakdown truck to tow your car and do whatever must be done. After dinner I will take you home to the chateau and all will be well.'

His sudden understanding made her blink fiercely as tears pricked her eyes, tears she rarely shed and would die rather than let fall. Were they because it was him? She didn't expect Raoul Giravel to show any softness — not to her, anyway!

Swiftly he moved all her precious parcels into his own, far larger boot, locked up and out of sight of any prying eyes or thieving hands.

With one light, encouraging touch on her shoulder, he settled her in his passenger seat. In silence they drove to St Cloud, where he drew up beside an ancient archway where it met the corner of a quiet market square.

A softly-lit, timbered restaurant beckoned Alex to enter and to eat — and eat well. Inside was comfort, shady lamps atop peach-coloured tablecloths, with tall green plants dotted here and there, lending an air of space and privacy.

The proprietor hurried to greet them, his chubby face wreathed in smiles. Obviously Raoul was a valued customer and she wondered how many other women he'd brought here. Shaking the thought away, she forced her shoulders to relax as he caught her elbow and they followed the patron to a secluded alcove.

Sinking onto a cushioned seat, Alex looked about her with a sigh of pleasure, but then caught sight of her grubby hands. Reasonably sure her face wasn't much better, she said, dismayed, 'I need to clean myself up. I must look awful.'

Raoul's hooded eyes lingered as though he had all the time in the world.

'You look beautiful,' he said slowly. 'But then, you always do. You must have been told so, many times, and by many men.' .

Leaning across the table, he stopped her indignant splutter by placing his fingers across her mouth. 'I am not trying to annoy you.' Then, 'By all means wash your hands. There is no hurry.'

Alex was determinedly brisk.

'You won't want to delay getting home, so if you'd like to save time and order something while I'm away, I promise I'll eat anything!'

The delicious aroma of cream and garlic wafted from plates a waiter was carrying to the only other diners, a couple who sat near the window. Alex couldn't stop the involuntary way the tip of her tongue touched her pink lips as she admitted, 'I'm absolutely starving. I'll only be a minute.'

Nodding, his mouth lifted in a half-smile.

'I quite like the grubby version of Mademoiselle Graham, but tidy yourself if you must.'

His soft chuckle followed as she made her way to the cloakroom.

Oh, he had charm, this wretched man! Cursing below her breath, she turned on the taps and then scowled at her dusty, dishevelled reflection. She was relieved that, for once, she'd chosen her favourite green sleeveless blouse and softly flared skirt instead of her usual more serviceable wear. With a tolerably clean face, she'd just about do — but only just!

Returning to their table, she found that Raoul had ordered their food, which soon arrived, accompanied by a bottle of wine. He poured a little into her glass and then held it to her lips.

'Drink! You need a few sips at least.' And then, gently once more, 'I think that you should let yourself relax just a little, knowing your parcels are safe, and that your interesting car will soon be ready to drive again.' He was unable to hide the teasing gleam in his eyes.

Alex's dimple came into play and her deep blue eyes sparkled as she found herself laughing at him across the table.

'Wretch! What did you do for entertainment before I came into your life?'

Amusement left his expression as, looking at his plate of tiny silver whitebait, he said, almost as though questioning himself, 'Before you came into my life? Little that mattered, apart from Lucie.' Absent-mindedly he broke a crusty roll and spread it with a curl of butter, but didn't start to eat. Instead his eyes returned to her face, as though trying to read her innermost thoughts.

'Lucie is a credit to you and your great-aunts,' said Alex, pushing away a tinge of discomfort as she felt the strength of his gaze. What was he thinking? What was he looking for? 'She and I spent quite a bit of time together when I collected the looms and needlework she and Silvie need for their display in the chateau.'

'Lucie greatly enjoys your company,' he said.

'Tell me how work is progressing at

your new project,' said Alex, embarrassed by the unspoken intensity of his look.

'Dessart's land?' It was as though she'd jolted him back to the present moment.

'You must stop calling it that,' she scolded. 'This is the new vineyard and it belongs to you!'

'I must remember!' At last his attention returned to his plate of food. 'If we are to talk about my new business, I might bore you with the story of biodynamic winemaking and the importance of working the land according to the seasons. There is nothing new about it, because everything is set in motion by Mother Nature.'

As he went on, enthusiasm lit his face in a way she'd not yet seen, even at Jenna and Luc's dinner, his, thoughts engrossed in describing what must be done. His whitebait demolished, he began tackling a plateful of duck, garnished with tiny truffles, which the waiter had just laid before him. It was almost as if he'd forgotten Alex was there. Digging his fork into a sliver of meat, he emphasised every word as if already working among the rows of vines he planned to grow.

'There's no time to lose! Some acres beside the riverbank have been resting for years but, in any case, my new plants will not need particularly good soil and one has to guard against making it too rich. A good vintage should come from having different varieties of grape working together.'

'Including those growing from the old Dessart roots?'

He nodded. 'Yes, there is no conflict. My main battle is to be constantly aware of the moon, how it waxes and wanes. I shall have different tasks that must be done at a certain time.' Excitement broke through again, his black eyes sparking with life in a way she found infinitely attractive.

Realising that, for this evening at least, he'd dropped his normal reserve,

Alex had to fight the urge to lean across the table and touch his strong jawline, her fingers moving slowly to his lips.

Mentally, she shook herself. *Come back to earth, girl! Yes, it's wonderful to share his vision of the future but it's all about bunches of grapes — not about Alex Graham!*

Doing her best to sound businesslike, she asked, 'Have you a name for the vineyard?'

'I am thinking . . . perhaps Domaine de Lucie.'

Alex clapped her hands in genuine pleasure.

'She'd love that!'

'She would insist on having your approval.'

Taken aback, Alex said, 'That's a great compliment. Thank you! But I doubt that my opinion would be of great account.'

He shook his head. 'You are wrong. You have crept into her heart.'

Suddenly adrift, Alex was momentarily silent. Then, once again, she led the conversation back to the practical.

'Did Lucie tell you we rode across your new land, right down to the river recently? She was asking about my work abroad, and then started hunting along the water's edge for Roman remains, perhaps even a villa! In the end she settled for some slivers of flint and insists they're prehistoric tools. I think you've a budding archaeologist on your hands!'

'I can think of worse occupations. Except that it would take her far from home. And I imagine that it will soon take you far away as well, when the tourist season ends here.'

Was there regret in his deep tone? Almost sombrely, he leaned back while the waiter removed their plates.

The dessert trolley brought back his smile because Alex couldn't hide her delight at the array of pastries, creams, trifles and fruit-filled tarts.

When she. had finally chosen, Raoul settling for cheese and biscuits, she answered.

'Yes, the East calls to me, although Mike, the friend whose book I was reading in Aix, says there's a place for me on his new dig in northern England. But since living in St Justin, only a few hours' drive from my family, I'm thinking of taking a closer look at excavations in France and the chance of getting a job. Around here, for instance, there's always the hope of finding wonderful caves — often, but not always, by accident.'

He nodded as she reminded him, 'Remember the grotto beneath the chateau — and there are Roman remains too. They're not particularly plentiful in this area but,' her dimples re-emerged, 'after Lucie's hunt for Early Man, and her interest in the whole thing, I've promised to take her to the Vesunna Museum. It's not far away and we'd both enjoy it. There are remains of an entire Roman villa there. You wouldn't mind me borrowing her for a day, would you?'

His eyes, almost tender, glinted.

'Have you not borrowed her suffi-ciently already?'

Not sure if he was joking, she tilted her head.

From across the table, he captured her hand.

'She loves you and it has not taken long for me to realise that others love you too.'

After a startled glance, she gently withdrew her fingers and they drank their coffee silently. She felt him take her hand again as they left the restaurant. As they walked to his car, Alex, had the strangest feeling of eyes watching her. Glancing back at the softly-lit building, she recognised a man at a table beside the window, staring at her.

Oops! Claude Jalabert! He'd assume that she'd cleared a space in her diary for Raoul Giravel — a space that she hadn't offered him.

Shrugging him from her mind, she sat in the darkness beside Raoul. The road leading from St Cloud appeared deserted as they drove away. With headlights turning dark lanes and grassy roadside to pale gold, a clear and starry night sky, the intimacy of Raoul's comfortable saloon made their silence warm and companionable. There was no need to speak.

Reaching the chateau, he drew up a few metres from the heavily studded main entrance. Sliding from his seat, he opened the passenger door, drew Alex slowly to her feet and into his arms.

As his lips, firm and warm, found hers, they demanded a response and she willingly gave everything he asked. In the moonlit courtyard, only a yard or so away the marble nymph, Celestine, was bathed in silver, an understanding and friendly presence.

For long moments, Raoul's mouth travelled smoothly across Alex's cheeks, her eyes, her neck, before returning to the curving lips which had enticed him from the moment they met at the bistro in Aix. His lean hands pulled her slim body even closer against the hard lines of his own.

Realising that at last he'd discarded the barrier of distrust he'd erected years ago, before they'd even met, Alex reached up and slid her arms around his neck. This was a moment she would treasure all her life, she thought, delighting in the touch of his jaw, the slight rasp of stubble on his strong chin, and the crisp dark hair that met the collar of his shirt.

At last he released her, his voice husky as he murmured 'We need to talk. But not tonight. I will see you tomorrow.'

Brushing her cheek against his before she stepped away, Alex whispered, 'Tomorrow.' As she moved to open the great door, he caught her in his arms again, as though he couldn't bear for her to go.

And then, with a final kiss and whispered 'Goodnight, Alexandrie Graham,' he paused only to make sure she was inside the main hall, before returning to his car and driving away.

It was hard to sleep. Was this the start of something wonderful? What did he want of her? Eventually she slid into dreams of an enigmatic, taut, sombre face that could break into a smile, a smile which had shown itself more often as the weeks had passed.

'Tomorrow,' she whispered once more into the night, happy in the certainty that he would come.

11

She was wrong. Next morning, instead of Raoul, one of the village boys appeared at the chateau with a note from him. In strong black handwriting, it told her that he'd been urgently called away to the vineyard at La Petite Grotte.

His manager there had overturned a small ride-on tractor they found necessary for working the narrow terraces. A broken leg and a cut arm would keep him at home for at least a few days, especially since the phone call from his wife had mentioned that he'd also suffered quite a bad knock on the head.

Typically brief, Raoul ended his two-line scrawl by saying that he would see Alex when he returned. There was nothing else, just his name.

Oh well! At least he'd told her why there'd be no sign of him today. Making a face at the wall, she called herself a fool for expecting more. What about something like *I will carry the memory of our evening with me . . .* or maybe one tiny kiss after the dark slash that spelled *Raoul?*

'One step at a time,' she muttered, swiping at a cobweb on the windowledge.

There wasn't even time for her to brood because the necklace was due from Paris any day, once security was assured. A specialist firm came to install the thick glass case in which it would stand, and an electrician experienced in setting up alarm systems would follow.

Alex needed to be at hand to make sure the case was placed in the right position, and found herself acting as coffee-server to the men setting up the heavy glass, and then to the two electricians who turned up within a few hours.

Madame Dupont had gone to visit her sister, Agnes, in Limeuil. She'd apologised for deserting Alex in her hour of need but the sister was unwell and she must go to check that neighbours were doing their best for her. In mid-morning she departed, her black straw hat set at an angle, with a jaunty yellow daisy stuck in the band.

The elder of the electricians introduced himself as Henri Lesage. Bald and fatherly, he was grateful for the coffee and cake Alex brought after he and his assistant had been working for a while.

Mug in one hand, with the other weaving circles he described the intricacies of the system being installed, obviously pleased by her interest. The opening mechanism would only be triggered from a control box in the cellar beneath the hall, from where a special circuit would monitor the entire building.

Apologising for their late arrival, he explained that his usual apprentice had suddenly been called away on family business.

'A nuisance just when I need him,

but can't be helped,' he said philosophically.

With a sideways wink and cautious nod in the direction of the younger man, Henri's voice dropped to a whisper. 'This chap's not a smiler but I only want an extra pair of hands, not a song-and-dance man!'

All in all, she felt reasonably confident the necklace would be in safe hands, especially when Henri said that only he and Alex would know the security number. It was a responsibility, but a sensible precaution.

'And you, mademoiselle, will have the only key to the cellar.' As he handed it to her, Alex felt this was a doubtful privilege but, later, from her office she glanced through the window overlooking the courtyard and chuckled.

'It's OK, Celestine — I'll look after it for you!' Was that a smile, or was it a shaft of sunlight striking the face of the marble nymph?

★ ★ ★

In late afternoon, when the phone rang, she expected to hear the museum in Paris asking when the work would be done, and the glass case ready for the jewels. Instead, it was a voice she hadn't expected to hear. Mike Delaney.

'Hi there, Alex!' He sounded as cheery as ever and, although she had enough work to keep her busy till midnight, she was glad to hear a familiar voice from her own, everyday working world.

'Just to warn you, I'll be down your way next week. That's when your exhibition opens, isn't it? I'd like to see what you've set up there, and I can usefully combine it with my annual stay with Bernard — you might remember I've a cousin who works at Versunna?'

Alex vaguely remembered Mike telling her he had a relation who, married to a French girl, had been lucky enough to land a behind-the-scenes job at the museum there.

'I'd love to see you Mike, and hear what you think of this place. And to catch up on all the dig gossip.'

'Plenty of that!' he said easily.

When she put the phone down, Alex found she was smiling. Mike invariably had that effect on her. This time, he'd not tried to flirt — it would be great if he was starting to notice there were girls in the world apart from Alex Graham.

★　★　★

The end of the week drew near but there was no word from Raoul. When Lucie and Silvie arrived to put the finishing touches to their craftwork display, they said he'd telephoned but couldn't leave La Petite Grotte for another day or so since there were a few complications with his manager's broken leg.

'Nothing serious,' said Lucie. 'But Papa wouldn't want to take any risks with Pierre's health. He's been with us for so many years that we think of him as family.'

Today, although Silvie protested that she was fit to walk the final slope to the chateau, knowing how busy Alex would be, they'd been driven the short distance to the village by their nearest neighbour, a retired office worker.

Although Alex longed for news of Raoul, she'd really hoped that they would bring a message meant for her alone. Or he could have telephoned her — even sent a one-line note.

'Nothing!' she muttered, slapping down a pile of visitor guidebooks with a force that sent dust flying in the pale golden light streaming through the open door of the main hall.

She had no shortage of visitors because Luc came for another flying visit, this time bringing with him Madeleine de Villiers, his sister-in-law, and ten-year-old Guy, who they jokingly referred to when he wasn't listening as 'lord of the chateau'.

'And of all its debts!' added Madeleine, pulling a wry face.

Alex had liked her immediately.

Guy's mother was petite, dark-haired and, though discreetly sophisticated, was charming too. She confided that, although her computer business in Paris was doing reasonably well, there was little spare cash remaining once living costs and school fees were paid.

'But we look to the future with confidence — just as my husband Alain always did.' Her face saddened as she glanced to where Guy was playing with two other boys, friends from the village. 'Alain would have been proud of our son.' She turned to Alex, a smile brightening her eyes.

'And now I need you to tell me what I can do to help! In no time at all, St Justin Week will arrive!'

Luc's role during his brief visit was to oversee preparations for safe and easy progress through the grotto, given the extra visitors, but then he was obliged to leave for Paris, promising to return towards the end of St Justin Week for a couple of days before taking Madeleine and Guy back with him.

'Jenna is terribly disappointed to miss all the fun,' he told Alex. A slight smile touched his lips as he added, 'You'll probably guess that I did my stern 'master of the house' performance to stop her hiding in the boot of the car!'

Although discharged from a short precautionary stay in hospital, Jenna had been forced to accept that the trip from Paris might be a risk.

Alex had been looking forward to the arrival of her mother in St Justin, but felt a tinge of apprehension when Eloise said her man friend, Christophe, would be coming too. They had decided to stay at the Auberge des Fleurs, where Eloise was already known to Elspeth and Philippe.

'You will have enough to cope with, cherie,' Eloise had explained when Alex expressed her dismay that she wouldn't be staying at the chateau. 'I telephoned Philippe and he has found rooms for Christophe and myself. I so much hope you will like him. He is a good man and we deal very well together.'

Alex, too, hoped she would like this first man in whom her mother had shown interest since her father's death. But as soon as she met Christophe, she was reassured.

Tall and slim, he had a scholarly air that went well with his short, greying sideburns, but there was kindness in his intelligent grey eyes. Alex warmed not only to his quiet sense of humour, but also to the affection in which he clearly held Eloise. If he eventually became part of their family, she need have no qualms. He had lost his wife several years ago and could understand that Alex's own father would always have a special place in her heart — but that there was room also for someone who cared about Eloise.

Her visitors found plenty to do because excitement had built to fever-pitch as the hours ticked past towards the start of St Justin Week. There were dozens of jobs to complete and willing hands were grabbed instantly. Strings of colourful bunting had to be hung across the river promenade, and draped around makeshift wooden stalls that were being loaded with trinkets for sale, as well as games to be played and prizes to be won. A tent for fortune-telling was there of course. If the black-garbed mystic had a look of Madame Clement from the boulangerie, no one would say a word! A podium had been erected for local dignitaries to stand on when the festival was officially opened, as well as scaffolding ready for a firework display on the final night.

A few yards along the riverbank there would be exhibitions of falconry, and an area reserved for donkey rides. On a concrete rectangle, normally a bicycle stand, a juggler and fire-eater would perform. This was Gizelle, a young woman from Sarlat. Clad in purple harem trousers, flame-coloured bolero and headdress, Alex had once seen her performing outside the cathedral.

Girls and boys from the school were rehearsing their singing and dancing at intervals through the day, and Alex felt an intense glow of pleasure as she spotted Madeleine helping with last-minute ideas for their fancy dress costumes, to be seen in all their glory on the final day's parade.

Alex had already hired temporary staff for the chateau, some to clean, and two local teenagers to keep the courtyard and its surrounds swept clear. Additionally, she'd found several women to take turns in the entrance kiosk, issuing tickets for the exhibition and grotto. Others would man a small stall with hot and cold drinks for anyone in need of a rest, but cheerful signs told visitors who wanted food that they'd find it in the cafes and bars which lined the village street.

Two days before the opening ceremony, Alex took a final look around the chateau, and — although she refused to admit it — a double look just to make sure the wonderful Oriental necklace would be safe once secured in its glass cabinet, before heading to her bedroom. Jenna had sent a typically funny illustrated note depicting a one-wheel trick cyclist with a puncture. The caption read 'Problems? What problems?'

Asleep almost as soon as her head touched the pillow, her lips curved as she murmured 'Roll on St Justin Week. Mission accomplished. Almost!'

Another sleepy whisper. 'Soon Raoul will be home . . . '

Would he think she'd done well? Had she, by some miracle, broken through that dark, silent reserve of his? And if she'd truly breached that final defence, the way into his heart, what next? Not an affaire, but something that would last. Surely his farewell kiss had been a silent promise?

12

Next morning, Alex was in the small room she used as an office, opening a stack of post which had arrived an hour ago.

The sun was shining, her exhibition was set up and ready for what Madame Dupont anticipated as a 'mass' of visitors, the riverbank festival site was prepared, would soon be en fete, and she'd never felt so happy in her entire life . . .

The door crashed open.

Raoul was there. He was in the grip of a fury she'd never met before. Not from anyone! Black eyes sparked disgust and disbelief as they met hers. In two long strides he dragged Alex to her feet. Cruel fingers bit into her arms.

'Why? Why did you do it?'

Throwing her aside, he strode from the room. The door slammed shut.

Sick and trembling, Alex clutched the edge of her desk. Then, rushing to the window, she saw his car, spurting showers of gravel as it roared from the courtyard. Skidding through the open gates, within seconds it was out of sight.

The door was flung open again. Madame Dupont ran into the room, her face ashen, every limb shaking.

'Mademoiselle! Are you hurt? Did he touch you?' Wringing her hands, she came to where Alex had sunk back into a chair. Putting both arms around the younger woman, she muttered 'Never have I seen such a rage!'

Stuttering outrage and shock, dismay and condemnation, she grabbed Alex and almost pushed her downstairs and into the kitchen. Quickly boiling the kettle, she filled a mug and put it in front of Alex, who sat at the table, face buried in both hands.

Unusually, the housekeeper had made herself a coffee at the same time but, after taking a few sips, set it down with a thud. She stood up and grabbed her coat from the hook. The look on her face dared anyone to stop her.

'I must hurry. I shall soon return. With news! I must discover why the Devil himself came to the chateau today!'

Alex didn't move, or respond. For the moment, the spark of defiance, always her instinctive defence, was dulled, even defeated. How could this be the Raoul who had kissed, caressed, even — perhaps — been within a whisper of loving her, scarcely more than a week ago?

Before an hour had passed, Madame Dupont returned. Alex was aimlessly rinsing their coffee mugs and staring sightlessly through the kitchen window, opened in the warm summer air. With both hands occupied, she didn't need to think. Even so, a tremor shook her limbs every so often.

'It is all around St Justin,' said the housekeeper, breathing heavily. Fit and energetic, in normal circumstances the climb downhill and a leisurely return created no difficulty. But today she had rushed both ways and now she fought for breath. Alex pulled forward a chair, urging her to sit.

'Take your time, Madame, or you'll be ill!'.

Still panting, the older woman shook her head as obediently she sat. She struggled to speak.

'Valuable Roman remains have been found on old Dessart's land, the vineyard that now belongs to Monsieur Giravel. The authorities have forbidden him to do more work there until they have investigated. Not one more spadeful, not even a snip with secateurs! It will take — who knows — how long? And Monsieur is beside himself with anger. He blames you, ma petite!'

Alex found her voice, though it came as a husky croak. 'Why me?'

'Because the pieces were left in a box outside the gendarmerie at Cahors of all places. It held a note to say they had been found by a resident who has a professional interest in such matters and lives close to the Giravel vineyard in St Justin!'

'I don't see why he assumes it was me!'

Madame Dupont's shrug was eloquent.

'Because you are an archaeologist, maybe? An expert in history? We have no one else of that description here!'

'An expert is the last person to dump Roman remains on someone's doorstep, for goodness' sake! Has Raoul gone mad?'

Thumping her fist on the table, Alex exploded at last, freed from the benumbing trance which had held her without thought, movement or feeling since Raoul's attack. 'I'm going to tackle him. This instant!'

Seeing the other woman's agitated face, it was Alex now who bent and put a comforting arm around the thin, black-clad shoulders.

'Don't worry, Madame! The only bandages you'll need will be for him. Not for me!'

It was a weak joke, but the best she could do to ease the strain. It worked, bringing a faint smile to the lined cheeks.

'I'll keep very calm, so don't fret. I'll merely ask Raoul why he should assume that I'm the culprit. Whistle-blower, I think they call it!'

Forcing a grin, she hurried away.

* * *

Where to find him? At the Dessart place? Or should she head for the gendarmerie in Cahors? The obvious, and nearest, was the holding that had been old Dessart's estate. Her car reached the entrance gates in seconds, or so it seemed to Alex, lost in anger, shock, and imagining what to say when she found Raoul.

No wonder she hadn't seen Lucie or Tante Silvie yesterday! It had crossed her mind that perhaps Raoul had returned to the cottage and they wouldn't want him to find it empty, with no food or welcome. Instead, they must have been forewarned of trouble, and prepared for the worst.

It was no good telling herself to keep calm! Injustice, especially from the man who'd haunted her dreams, lit a spark to fury. Fiery curls, vividly blue flashing eyes, and determined chin spoke of the fight to come.

She saw him. He was walking among the old vines. Wrenching the wheel, she charged across pitted soil, along furrows, stones spraying in all directions. Reaching him, she slithered to a halt, leaping out almost before the car stopped.

'So what was all that about, you moron?' she shouted. 'I know what you're thinking! The entire village knows what you're thinking!' Hands on hips, feet apart, she faced him like a small tornado. 'Why the devil d'you think I'd do a sneaky thing like that?'

'Because you care for nothing and no one but yourself!' Flinging down his heavy stick, Raoul strode to meet her.

Standing inches away, he towered over Alex's slight, furious figure. 'You told me you showed Lucie how to search for finds! She was happy with a few stones. But what did your own eyes see?'

As she opened her mouth for a cutting retort, his black eyes darted arrows of steel. One contemptuous gesture dismissed anything she would say.

'You told me the two of you were looking along the river. Did you scuff the dirt with your hands? What did your sharp eyes see? Did you satisfy Lucie with a useless piece of rock?' Questions ricocheted like bullets. Leaning even closer, his breath scorched Alex's cheek.

'Did you sneak back, alone, for a second look? And you found something! But any decent person would have told me! You knew I would soon be with you again. Instead you rushed to the authorities. One small scrap of shame, or more probably a lifetime's skill in deception, made you hide your identity!'

Breathing fast, he spat words between his teeth.

'A coward as well as a traitor! Did you not think to take me to the place where they were buried, and allow me the dignity of reporting them? The Ministry, the museum, the archaeologists? Why did you crawl like some scurvy snake straight to the police, who now suspect me of hiding them!'

As Alex opened her mouth, he bent forward to place a hard hand across her lips.

'I made no secret of my plans when we talked. You know full well that, in this vineyard, time and the seasons are vital. Any fool knows that delay can mean the end of my hopes, my dreams and, with it, financial ruin!'

Stepping back at last, his lean face was filled with scorn. Alex felt the breath knocked out of her body. 'You are like all the rest of your sex. Betrayal feeds the blood in your veins. For a time I imagined you might be different.' He laughed bitterly. 'I was wrong! Now get off my land!'

Reason was useless. Alex didn't even try. She spread her hands in an expression of helplessness, flung herself into the car and drove off. She would see if Silvie or Lucie were at the Huilier cottage.

Arriving at the shabby little building, she hesitated, then accelerated away. It wouldn't be fair to draw them, especially Lucie, into this.

She didn't doubt they'd accept her word that she had nothing to do with it. With Raoul being convinced that she'd played some dreadful trick on him, they'd have divided loyalties. No, she must find the truth some other way.

One thing was painfully clear. What she'd imagined as a softening in Raoul's attitude was no more than skin-deep. Beneath the surface, he was as raw and distrustful as ever. Her throat ached as she brushed a hand across her eyes. Now it was her turn for some distrust. Had he been setting her up for a nice little fling? A nice little overnight stay, or perhaps two, a few miles away where no one would know them?

In the chateau, the phone was ringing as she hauled herself up the curving iron banisters and reached her office. A shaft of comfort warmed her chilled nerves as she recognised the caller.

'Mike!' Mike Delaney, who would never in a million years doubt her. Suddenly, tears began to roll down her face as he explained the reason for his call.

'I'm actually already in the Vesunna area with Bernard. I got away from the dig sooner than expected and Bernard's wife is happy for me to stay at their place again. Seemed the perfect chance to come and see what you're up to.'

'I'd like that, Mike.' Unable to hide the husky note in her voice, she should have known that Mike would pick up on it.

'Hey Alex! What's the matter, my love?'

'Just something that came up today.

Led to a rotten bust-up. You know what a wimp I am — hate trouble, day or night! It's nothing to worry about.'

'I might disagree about that,' said Mike slowly. 'It's not like you to sound so upset.' He paused for a moment. 'Look, I've got to go now, but I'll ring you first thing tomorrow. And if you don't answer, I'll come and get you. I can't have some local lout upsetting one of my women!'

Despite her misery, a gurgle of laughter escaped from Alex.

'That's better! Cheer up, old dear. We'll speak again, first thing tomorrow morning. OK?'

As Mike rang off, Alex heard voices outside the open window and sighted a small security van. Beside it was Madame Dupont on the chateau steps, issuing instructions.

The Oriental necklace had arrived. The necklace that Marcel, the young lord, had brought home for poor, tragic Celestine.

For the next few hours there was no

time to think about Raoul or to wonder what mischief had been set in motion, and by whom. Despite the desolation in her heart, she had a job to do. As curator of the museum, and instigator of its exciting new exhibition, she, and she alone, was responsible for the priceless jewellery.

A strong rectangular table had been set up as a centrepiece in the main hall. On it stood a display case of reinforced glass in which the jewels would be housed. Its metal framework was constructed so that one glass panel could be opened. Soon, Alex was arranging the precious stones on the dark blue velvet background she'd agreed with Luc and Jenna. Henri, the electrician, had already fitted tiny spotlights inside the case, and now they endowed each separate gem, with a fiery, glorious life of their own.

Henri had arrived earlier, waiting to activate the alarm system. It took a while but, once he and the security team were satisfied, eventually Alex could relax. Only then did she realise that for the past couple of hours she'd been clenching her hands, and casting nervous glances at innocent shadows in corners of the empty exhibition hall.

'The case can only be opened by remote control. Be assured of that, mademoiselle!' Henri stood back from the display with a satisfied sigh, and rubbed the palms of his hands down the legs of shabby dungarees. 'Remember that you and I alone know the combination to operate the release. And only you have a key, and a new lock, for the cellar.' His hearty laugh rang around the wooden ceiling rafters as, casting a glance at Alex's anxious face, he laid his stubby hand on her shoulder. 'Have no fear! All will be well!'

Her next visitor was an officer who introduced himself as Inspector George Vincent from the gendarmerie in St Cloud. A short, thick-set man, with piercing grey eyes, she liked him and his obvious competence. His men would be on duty in the village, their numbers increased by others who might be spared from Sarlat, but nonetheless he was concerned that security beyond the promenade area would still only be minimal. Alex showed him a plan which illustrated the layout of the building. Fortunately none of the downstairs windows could be opened and, as for doors, there were only two — the main double door at the front, and just one entrance at the rear.

'It's the old postern gate,' she said, leading him around the courtyard to where a small, stout wooden door was located almost two metres above ground level. It could only be reached via a narrow wooden staircase, one which in ancient times could be removed at the first hint of attack. 'We mostly use it for deliveries — groceries and suchlike — and it's always locked and bolted on the inside.'

Satisfied, the Inspector departed.

★　★　★

It was a pity that Luc and Jenna couldn't be here for the celebration week. When Luc had come for his brief overnight stay, he'd brought another huge parcel of heraldic standards and banners, so now the grey stonework acted as the perfect foil to brilliant silks and braids. He'd been delighted with Alex's work in the chateau and particularly interested in the Library where she had set out a fine, illustrated account of the Crusaders, and the families they'd left behind in the medieval village.

'This display is something we can keep long after St Justin's Week is done and dusted,' he'd said. 'It'll be an extra attraction over the years — and every coin that safeguards young Guy's inheritance is desperately needed!'

As Alex, standing beside Madeleine and Guy, waved him goodbye, she prayed that Luc's optimism wouldn't be disappointed. She'd done everything humanly possible to make the next week and the rest of the summer a success. Surely nothing could go wrong?

13

Early on Saturday, the entire village was awake and outdoors soon after dawn. Excited children ran along the promenade, and small groups of bartenders and cafe owners had an extra air of urgency as they set out tables on the pavement.

It was going to be a warm day, drenched with sunshine. What more could they ask for? Apart from lots of visitors, of course!

Their hopes were soon realised as people started swarming into the riverbank area, by bus, an assortment of private cars and many on foot. For those who didn't relish the climb to the chateau, Jacques Cours, owner of the canoe business, had loaned a small minibus and insisted that the driver and all the fuel were his contribution to the festival. For those with more severe mobility problems, a small area at the rear of the building had been set aside as a special car park and a temporary ramp also installed beside the three shallow entrance steps to the main hall.

Above the busy promenade, the chateau and its temporary staff were sharing the promenade's excitement. Mostly local housewives and students, they'd been keen to wear medieval clothes. Rather than go to the expense of hiring costumes, they'd asked Alex to find pictures of gowns the villagers might have worn in those days.

'Simple and modest,' she suggested. 'They would have been hardworking peasants. But we won't insist on goat wool cloth, unless someone finds us a truckload of goats!'

Some of the local men jokingly agreed 'to make fools of ourselves'. They wouldn't need chainmail tunics and metal helmets like the two life-size display models of knights, borrowed by Luc for the museum, so contriving ordinary soldiers' costumes had been reasonably easy. As with the women's gowns, historical accuracy quite often had to take a back seat. Quietly amused, Alex suspected that Richard the Lionheart, recruiting his Crusaders, might have raised his eyebrows!

A cheer and fanfare of trumpets from the promenade announced that St Justin's Week was officially open, and a second cheer echoed from her small army inside the chateau.

Alex couldn't help being caught up in such a happy atmosphere and perhaps only Madame Dupont guessed that her spirits were as heavy as lead. The housekeeper had returned from Limeuil, reassured that her sister was being cared for, and hinted that she had some interesting news to pass on when time allowed. Alex had hidden a smile. The little woman never failed with her information network!

Thomas, the carpenter, having finished the wooden ramp alongside the entrance steps, turned his mind to smaller projects. Soon his worktable was covered with small ornaments, some sold to his audience as soon as he'd finished carving them. There was plenty more entertainment for them because other twelfth-century crafts such as pottery, jewellery-making and willow basket weaving soon attracted customers.

In the Library, the school's art mistress was inscribing a fresh, illustrated manuscript, even using gold leaf as the monks might have done. Soon, too, lively notes issued from a corner where the music teacher was making flutes.

The workroom prepared for Lucie and Silvie to demonstrate their crafts was empty, their tapestry canvases and weaving loom standing idle.

Biting her lip, Alex turned away. What else had she expected? But, even as she walked back through the hall and down the steps to the courtyard, a familiar black saloon drew to a halt. Looking straight ahead behind the steering wheel sat Raoul.

Quickly the car doors opened. Lucie ran to throw both arms around Alex and give her a bear-hug, something she'd never done before. Touched beyond words, Alex hugged her back and turned to greet Silvie who came and kissed her on both cheeks before discreetly squeezing her hand. Their silent support brought suspicious moisture to Alex's eyes and quickly she brushed it away.

A remote voice came from where Raoul was taking a wooden frame from the boot of the saloon where, a lifetime ago, Alex had felt cared for and perhaps even thought she might be taking the first steps into a new and special phase in her life. Ignoring her, he spoke to Lucie.

'Gilbert will collect you when he finishes work at five o'clock. Do not keep him waiting!'

The harsh line of his jaw was that of a stranger. It was hard for Alex to believe that, one magical evening, she had smoothed it with her hand, as he drew her close to his lithe body.

For one fleeting second his eyes narrowed as though he, too, was remembering. If regret was in that dark gaze it vanished before he eased his long frame into the driving seat. A closer look might have revealed unhappiness and loss.

As he turned on the ignition, a low-slung sports car drove through the entrance gates and came to rest beside Alex. A tall, thick-set man with a mop of curly fair hair jumped out.

'Alex! Hello, darling!'

She was lifted of her feet and clasped in strong, masculine arms, while a smacking kiss was planted on each cheek.

'Mike! I didn't expect you!' Alex struggled to get free. 'But put me down so I can breathe!'

'Sorry, love! Call it joie de vivre at the sight of my favourite girl!'

She tried to smile but, secretly dismayed, saw Raoul watching, stony-faced. But first, surely there was a shadow of feeling? And now it was too late. His lip curled. His engine roared into life. And then he'd gone.

Mike waved down the driver of the sports car, which had been turning, ready to drive away again.

'Nicole, hang on a minute while I introduce Alex!' Quickly he explained that the woman behind the wheel worked with his cousin Bernard and had offered him a lift.

'Nicole knew I was keen to see you today. She'll pick me up in a couple of hours and then we're heading to a place I'm interested in, where she's an appointment later. Something to do with computers scanning the more fragile artefacts.'

Nicole was a cheery brunette with friendly brown eyes. She called a smiling 'Hi, Alex!' and mouthed a quick promise to come and meet properly, before driving off.

Lucie and Silvie had started climbing the steps, each carrying the medieval costume they would wear. In her spare hand Lucie also held the wooden frame that Raoul had taken from the car boot. As Mike and Alex caught up with them, he relieved them of their parcels. Uncertainly, they thanked him but then looked questioningly at Alex. Briefly she introduced Mike as a friend from England.

'You remember, the one who sent me the Merlin book,' she reminded Lucie. So much had happened since they first met at the bistro in Aix and now wasn't the time to ask the teenager what was happening at the vineyard. She knew Mike well enough to guess he'd already picked up some undercurrents.

He spent a few minutes chatting in his easy way as they went into what they called 'the tapestry room'. Alex was glad to hear Lucie laugh as she told him how she'd puzzled over his 'trowel' inscription on the flyleaf.

Leaving them to don their costumes, he came back to the grand hall. Slowly turning his head from side to side, he let out a low whistle.

'Wow, Alex! This is really something! I'll enjoy having a good look around. I can see you've put a ton of work into this lot.' He lightly took her hand as she led him towards the main staircase and headed for the gallery. Lowering his voice, he said, 'But, before that, I want to know who or what's upsetting you. And why the atmosphere between you and the two ladies down there — ' he nodded in the direction of the tapestry workshop — 'was strained, to say the least!' Glancing sideways at her set expression, he added, 'Not to mention their chauffeur. My limbs have turned to ice!'

'It's a long story, Mike,' said Alex, waving him to the larger of the two chairs as they went into her office. 'I've got to find what's behind it, but someone's been making mischief and I've unwittingly become the fall-guy.'

Describing Raoul as a new neighbour, she related what she knew of the detailed plans he'd made to create a biodynamic vineyard which he would work alongside older vines he'd taken over from the Dessart years. Her eyes brightened as she described how she and his daughter, Lucie, had become friends.

'We spent quite a bit of time together and she loved hearing about some of the digs I'd worked on. One day when we were out riding, she got it into her head that we might find archaeological remains along her father's riverbank.'

Mike grinned as Alex recounted Lucie's insistence that she'd found an Iron Age knife made of flint.

His face straightened as she told him how a box of pottery fragments, supposedly from the vineyard, had been dumped outside the gendarmerie, with a note hinting that a specialist in ancient remains was responsible for finding them. As Alex had done, Mike exploded.

'What complete tripe! As if anyone — let alone you — anyone who knew the first thing about history would dump Roman remains on anyone's doorstep!' Scuffing an irate hand through his hair, he was silent, a frown creasing his forehead.

'We must find out exactly what the box held. For starters, we want to know if the 'remains' are genuine. Or merely Auntie Mavis's vase that some idiot's dropped.' His frown deepened. 'Sounds to me like an almighty hoax. Worse, it sounds like someone wants to louse up this chap Raoul's vineyard business before he's even started.'

Pushing back his chair, he wandered over to the window and looked out, but Alex knew he wasn't seeing anything below.

'You're sure that whatever was written seems aimed at you?' She reluctantly nodded. 'I assume you can't think of anyone else it might be?' Seeing Alex shake her head, he went on. 'If you're right, I'd guess that some rotten skunk doesn't like you much, my old dear!'

Alex was relieved that he accepted her word — and that, apart from that

Mike-like greeting, there was no sign of anything deeper. Anyone watching and listening would instantly register him as one of Alex's good pals — nothing more.

She guessed that Mike's quick eyes had registered particular tension between herself and Raoul, even in that brief courtyard encounter, but was relieved that, learning at least part of the reason, he made no comment.

Taking him down to the kitchen, she introduced him to Madame Dupont, who offered coffee and a huge slab of her latest gateau. Swallowing the final mouthful, he told her it was wonderful, and though this was just a brief visit, he'd be back to see her in a couple of days. 'If I'm lucky, you'll have a slice left — a large one!' he joked in quite passable French and, beaming, the housekeeper assured him he wouldn't go hungry.

'I'd better go outside and wait for Nicole,' he told Alex. 'The chap she's seeing is a dab hand at computer analysis and she thought I'd like to hear what he's up to, so we'll have to rush off.'

He ruffled Alex's hair as they reached the courtyard, and gave her a quick hug. 'I'm getting an idea re what to do with your Roman stuff. Uncle Mike's on the case.' Adopting a heavy Scottish accent, he said 'Dinna fash yersel' lassie!'

Giggling, Alex aimed a mock slap at his arm as Nicole drove through the gates.

'Idiot!' she told him, waving at the other girl. 'You might dig for years near Hadrian's Wall, but you'll never make a Scotsman. Best to stay south, in case an Ancient Pict comes and grabs you!' It was wonderful to laugh again.

When they'd gone, she felt as though a weight had been lifted from her shoulders. It was enough just to feel that a friend like Mike, and others too, would dismiss as ludicrous any idea of her as a mischief-maker. As for Raoul and his savage condemnation — again she asked herself, how could there ever be love if there was no trust? And it seemed that trust was something which held no place in his heart. It was better to give herself a good shake and forget those half-formed dreams. If only she could . . .

Returning to the kitchen, Alex thanked Madame Dupont for the welcome she'd given Mike, and sat down for another cup of coffee.

'There hasn't been a chance to tell you about the day I visited my sister,' the housekeeper said, clearly dying to relate the latest gossip. 'Apparently, on the bus to Limeuil, she'd sat next to a woman who worked for Auguste Jalabert at the Coq d'Or hotel. It seems there was a most terrible, terrible commotion the previous day. Auguste was shouting in a way no one had ever heard! The woman said he'd almost screamed 'Get out of my hotel!''

'Who was he shouting at?' asked Alex, curious because it was hard to imagine the apparently jovial 'Santa

Claus' losing his cool, much as she disliked him.

'Why, Claude, of course! Who else?' Madame Dupont folded her arms across her flat chest. Leaning forward, her voice a confidential whisper, despite the kitchen being empty, 'Everyone knows Claude has gambling debts. It is thought that in the past his father settled them. But this time Claude promised payment in return for a favour — I do not know what. These people are still waiting for the money. They are threatening him. And so are others. It has come to the ears of Auguste and he is beside himself with anger!'

Grimly smiling, she added, 'He was already furious that, when he sent Claude to buy old Dessart's land, the fool was too late. Probably wasting time at the races!' She slapped her hand on the table, careless of Alex's empty mug as it jumped. 'Claude is caught in a nasty circle of gamblers, and such men become dangerous!'

'That might explain why neither of them — has shown his face here to see what's going on,' realised Alex. Without exception, the rest of the festival committee had visited, some even this morning taking time to wander around the museum, exclaiming and congratulating her on a job well done. They were intrigued by the marvellous necklace but, even now, she couldn't bring herself to admit that, until it was safely back in Paris, she'd be scared to let it out of her sight, unless her small army of carers was on guard.

The germ of an idea had filtered into her mind as Madame Dupont talked about Claude, bringing a memory of him rushing past the bistro in Aix, on his fruitless mission to the notaire's office. For the moment, she brushed it away. It was too outrageous. All the same, she might take it out and play around with a few thoughts later.

* * *

213

An exciting phone call came during the afternoon, even though it brought some disappointment. Luc rang to say that he couldn't come to the festival, even for another flying visit. Jenna was in hospital, the baby's arrival imminent though slightly premature. He would stay with her until Michel's brother or sister was born and would need to be at home while the family got used to its new regime and he was satisfied that Jenna was completely fit.

Alex was happy to know their long wait was nearly over and asked Luc to give Jenna her love and best wishes. It would be lovely to see them again soon, this time with two children instead of one. She loved being an honorary aunt to Michel but couldn't ignore a tiny pang. Would she ever have children of her own?

A vision of a small boy with unruly black curls and dark eyes popped into her mind, a boy who walked tall, with the unconscious near-arrogance of his father. Irritably she swatted a fly from her desk, doubly irritated when she missed it.

In the meantime, after the firework display next Saturday, Madeleine must return to Paris, since she couldn't leave her business for too long. In Luc's absence, she and Guy would hire a car to take them home, but at least they'd be here for the final celebration.

It had been a whirlwind few hours, decided Alex, feeling as though she'd run a marathon, and the next couple of days would be even busier.

Five o'clock arrived and Raoul's man, Gilbert, came to collect Lucie and her great-aunt. As they came down the steps to the car, they thanked Alex for giving them a lovely day.

'People were so interested in watching us work the loom, and quite a few tried to do tapestry work.' Lucie was bubbling with enthusiasm. She looked charming, thought Alex, in her long blue dress with fitted sleeves, a girdle around her hips and her long brown hair partly covered with a medieval wimple in fine white cloth.

'Aunt Marthe is driving herself here one day this week. She wants to see the new land we own, and enjoy a few hours of carnival. My aunt knew the chateau when she was younger, and is looking forward to visiting your exhibition,' she said, noticeably omitting any mention of Raoul. Tentatively raising a hand, Lucie gently touched Alex's cheek. 'Sleep well tonight, ma chere amie!'

Sleep well! Some hopes! The problem wasn't just an attractive Frenchman with the wildness of the Camargue about him. She had already discovered that another, insistent unease meant there could be no undisturbed rest.

* * *

As midnight approached, once again Alex swung her feet out of bed and grabbed her dressing gown. It was no good. Whatever reassurances Henri the electrician had given her, however strong the glass showcase, she and she alone was responsible for Celestine's necklace — those fabulously precious stones with their unique and intricate gold setting.

There was only one dim light at the foot of the main staircase as she headed for the Library where a velvet-covered couch stood against one wall, a small notice asking visitors not to sit there. Upstairs, she'd grabbed her usual cushion and blanket, and now she settled herself. It wasn't too uncomfortable a way to spend the night because, even as she berated herself for a ridiculous fear, comfort came from being near the jewels. Always a light sleeper, with the door slightly ajar, the smallest sound in the grand hall would wake her.

Beneath the portrait of St Justin, Alex slept.

14

Dawn had scarcely broken but Raoul was unconscious of the slight breeze, the clear air which heralded a beautiful day, the birdsong or the flutter of wings as he trudged through the old vineyard and headed towards the area where he'd planned to create his new venture near the riverbank.

Already, the archaeologists had cordoned off a substantial area of flat ground and pegged out what he assumed were specific lanes for a group of field-walkers and later, perhaps, ground-searching radar equipment.

In truth, his first explosive rage was blunted now he'd accepted the delay, even the wrecking, of plans that had excited him like a child. As well as disappointment, he'd face financial difficulty he could ill afford if planting was seriously delayed, or if it even

218

became impossible. He'd tried hard to reason with himself. Everyone encountered setbacks from time to time! If he'd been the one to find Roman remains near the river, he would have reported them too, whatever the consequences to himself.

Different altogether was someone who'd searched his land, found something, and taken it to the authorities — anonymously at that! Why not tell him first? The whole business reeked of deliberate trespass, discovery, and deceit.

Blocking her face from his mind didn't work. Hurt and betrayal forced its way through, colouring his image of Alex.

Instinct whispered that she was as true as steel. But what about logic? He'd learned cruel lessons in the past. How could he forget that a woman's looks counted for nothing? All her glorious golden hair, those deep blue eyes, the dimple beside kissable pink lips was a cover for deception. She'd the strength for it, a defiance that attracted, as much as it tantalised him.

Was he being unfair? Jumping to conclusions? Shaking his head, mechanically Raoul pushed back the dark, untidy curls from his forehead. No. She'd as much as admitted her guilt at dinner that unforgettable night when he'd believed that, finally, he held in his arms the woman he had been unknowingly waiting for.

She'd told him how she and Lucie rode along the riverbank. He'd laughed with her when she described how Lucie searched for signs of ancient life. It must have been Alex who, spotting pottery fragments, said nothing but secretly returned later, alone.

Why she'd gone straight to the authorities he could only guess. Did she distrust him as much as he now distrusted her? Did she think he'd want to hide her find, keep it quiet, cover it with new vines? To her, an archaeologist by profession, that would be unthinkable!

Drawing a deep breath, Raoul slowed his steps through the dusty soil. Thrusting both hands through his hair, unconsciously pressing the hard bones of his skull, he looked to where the river flowed towards the distant sea.

How big a fool could a man be? To fall in love and to want no one but this woman! Stretching out, he grabbed a broken branch, and savagely thrashed a clump of undergrowth. Hurling the branch into the water, he watched the current snatch and toss it downstream.

By the time he returned to the Huilier cottage, Lucie was helping Silvie lay the table for breakfast. Her glance was uncertain as Raoul walked into the small kitchen, and quickly she read the strain around his mouth.

They ate and drank in silence. For the past few days Gilbert, Raoul's groundsman, had driven them to the museum to save the short walk, and collected them later, but today he was occupied elsewhere, so Raoul was their unwilling chauffeur.

'If you wish me to take you to the chateau, I shall leave in five minutes,' he warned, pushing aside his half-eaten croissant. 'I do not know when Tante Marthe will arrive today so I have given her a spare key to the cottage.'

Lucie and Silvie were waiting beside the car when he came through the gate. As they arrived outside the chateau, Lucie, despite Raoul's ominously black mood, gathered courage before she began to climb the steps.

'Papa, it is almost the end of St Justin's Week. Will you not come and look at Alex's exhibition? It is fascinating! I know you would be interested. She has done well!'

'I have no wish to admire the skills of someone so talented in deception.'

He didn't try to hide his contempt. Words were the only way for him to disguise the disillusionment that, for years, had seared his heart. Haunting him, too, was the sight of Mike clasping Alex, comfortably familiar in a way Raoul couldn't imagine for himself.

Once she was alone with her English archaeologist friend, how soon would that embrace turn to something more?

He didn't notice Alex standing beside Celestine's statue. She had been enjoying a quiet moment before the day grew busy. Now, scarcely able to believe Raoul's condemnation, she confronted him, almost incandescent with rage.

'Are you referring to me, Monsieur Giravel? Or should I address you as Bigoted Oaf?' Blue eyes blazing, her insult sliced the air.

'Why do you not face the truth? Taken aback, after one second Raoul glared at her before his mouth thinned to a sarcastic line. 'Admit it! That deceit comes naturally to such as you!'

As Alex opened her mouth, ready to erupt, Lucie, frozen in dismay, suddenly sprang to life. She grabbed Alex's hand.

'Alex, Papa doesn't mean what he says!'

'Lucie! Be quiet!' snapped Raoul. 'This is no business of yours!'

His words were the spark to a tinder-box. Clenching her fists, the girl sprang forward, beating him on the chest. Astounded, Raoul tried to catch her hands as, off-balance, he fell back several paces.

Still attacking, sobbing hysterically, Lucie screamed at him, leaving them all stunned.

'Deceit? How can you talk to me of deceit? When you are not even my father!'

A deadly silence fell. Then a low, horrified moan came from Silvie's ashen lips. An imploring hand begged Lucie to say no more, her agonised eyes revealing the truth. The girl ran to bury her face in the little woman's shoulder.

Raoul, grey-faced beneath his tan, threw open the car door, bundling Lucie and his aunt back inside. For one fleeting second he glanced over his shoulder. Alex had no chance to hide the stricken look in her eyes. Already she'd been hurt beyond belief, devastated by his accusation, and now utterly shocked by Lucie's words.

Raoul's own face changed. Instinct was crying to him, begging him to defy all reason. Suddenly, unbelievably, remorse shadowed his eyes.

'Alex, what I have done to you! Forgive me!' He held out his hand but then, torn between her and Lucie, had to let it fall and turn back to the sobbing girl.

Tears were running down Alex's face as, knowing she couldn't take any more, she shook her head and ran silently into the safety of the chateau.

★   ★   ★

What had Lucie meant? There was no chance to think because already the day's first minibus of tourists was drawing up outside the building. However much she longed for time and space to relive and try to understand that devastating disclosure, she had responsibilities.

As usual, firstly she needed to check

that her temporary staff of 'peasants' had turned up and direct them to good vantage points. In the Library she needed someone particularly reliable to watch that no curious fingers touched fragile manuscripts displayed there.

It wasn't until early evening that her mind was free to replay the scene over and over, without finding an answer. Raoul's and his aunt's horrified reactions confirmed the truth. Lucie was not his daughter.

Even Raoul's parting words held no comfort. They seemed to be telling her that he'd been wrong, that in his heart he believed her innocent. So what? Tiredly, Alex knew she was almost past caring. Suddenly the weight of the summer had caught up with her.

The responsibility of the chateau, the mountain of organisation and creativity she'd brought to the exhibition, the excitement and then the despair of loving Raoul, his lack of trust and now the revelation that he was not, in fact, Lucie's father. If he'd changed his mind about Alex's role in the Roman pottery debacle — well, again, so what? *Love hurts*, she thought wearily. *Isn't that what people say? Well, they're right!*

There was no sign of Lucie or her aunt the following day, or the next. Even if Marthe had arrived at the Huilier cottage, Alex didn't expect to see her either. As for Raoul, all his emotions and energies would have to be spent reassuring Lucie that nothing had changed, and revealing the truth surrounding her birth. The bond of affection between them couldn't be fatally damaged by Lucie's revelation, could it? Blood tie or no blood tie, it would surely make no difference — but they had so much to discuss, to grow used to their new relationship, and that would take time.

Desperately Alex trawled her mind for other images, everyday happenings that might penetrate this black cloud of confusion, desolation and misery. Forcing a smile was so difficult. The best thing to do, she found, was to look, and be, constantly busy.

At least the week brought some moments of light relief. A lively party of Girl Guides had been intrigued by the chain-mailed figures, but perhaps even more so by the bizarre length of a garish scarf being knitted by Madame Clement's mother, who was happy to sit for a few hours and keep guard. Needles clicking, she'd let her imagination soar into fantasy land with colourful tales of Crusading knights who once rode through the village. Recommending a leading brand of silver cleaner used, she insisted, by their squires to clean the metal helmets, she didn't notice the girls' giggles.

Henri Lesage, the electrician, brought his wife and made sure she admired his spotlights in the display case quite as much, if not more, than the valuable necklace. Three young children escaped their parents while he was there, running the length of the hall until his booming voice warned them to play outside. Their embarrassed parents emerged from the Library, adding scolding to the commotion.

Alex's mother, Eloise, with her beau Christophe, had come to see the museum on the first day, and had returned for several hours. Both had extensive knowledge of medieval history, which gave their generous praise extra meaning for Alex. The tiny chapel with its ornate carvings and its walls decorated with frescoes, surprisingly bright even though centuries had passed, captured their attention in particular.

'What a wonderful setting for a wedding,' laughed Eloise. 'Luc will be hoping Guy finds himself a nice girl when he's older, so that it can be seen in its glory again.'

They went on to enjoy Alex's informal tour of the family's private rooms, ending once again in the kitchen. As with Mike, Madame Dupont plied them with coffee and patisserie in between loading a pannier with biscuits needed for the small snack bar located in an annexe at the rear of the hall. She seemed to have boundless energy and was revelling in all her extra tasks.

Alex couldn't join her mother and Christophe for dinner at the Auberge des Fleurs, but they understood her reluctance to leave the building in the evening, even if Madame Dupont was upstairs in her small apartment.

Eloise made Alex promise that, once Celestine's jewels went back to Paris, they'd spend time together before she returned home to Aix, with Alex following at the end of summer.

At the Auberge, Eloise must have heard gossip, about Raoul's vineyard and the wrecking of any romance with her daughter but, thank goodness, made no comment. Instead, in her quiet way, she showed support for everything that Alex had achieved, including her obvious popularity with the residents of St Justin.

Luc, in his latest phone call, had said that Gertrud, his regular curator, would be free to return when Alex decided it was time to leave. Soon, the school's autumn term would begin, the village returning to normal.

The more Alex saw of Christophe, the more she liked him. He was an intelligent and interesting man, and when she heard him laughing with Eloise and watched the tenderness in his eyes, she was hopeful that her mother wouldn't spend any more years alone.

Soon after they left to watch a falconry display on the promenade, Mike walked in, accompanied by Nicole and his cousin, Bernard. Around all three hovered an air of suppressed excitement. Could Alex take them somewhere to talk privately?

Upstairs, in her office, they told her they'd been asked by the Cultural Department to examine what they called 'Raoul's pottery' in Bernard's museum laboratory.

'I smelt a rat as soon as he opened the box,' said Mike, with a satisfied grin. 'And these two confirmed it.'

'We identified one piece as a lamp which went missing from an excavation in Provence,' added Nicole, her brown eyes sparkling. 'Fragments of a decorated vase came from Ampurias in Spain. We looked up other computer records and eventually matched an intricate brooch to one inexplicably stolen two years ago from a laboratory in Greece.'

As Alex's eyes filled with tears of relief, Nicole threw both arms around her. 'So you have no more need to worry. This was a deliberate effort, incredibly ignorant and crude, to cause trouble for Monsieur Giravel.' She dropped a kiss on Alex's wet cheek before adding, 'For you also.'

'Have you told Raoul?'

'Yes, we actually went to find him at his other vineyard this morning. He was overwhelmed with relief but insists the field team continue their work on his new land at St Justin for as long as necessary, to make certain it is completely clear.'

'Apart from young Lucie's Iron Age knife, of course,' added Mike with his usual good humour. 'The police are working on a tip-off but being pretty tight-lipped about their suspicions.' Tilting his head slightly to look at Alex with keen eyes, he added, 'Raoul seemed anxious that you should know before anyone else.'

He didn't add that he wondered why Raoul hadn't already driven back to the village, or at least telephoned, to offer Alex abject apologies. Grateful for Mike's understanding, she suggested they adjourn to the kitchen to celebrate.

After yet another coffee with Madame Dupont, who they swore to at least temporary secrecy with the news, they spent time looking around the rooms and then, accepting that Alex couldn't join them, drove off to eat at one of Bernard's favourite restaurants a few miles away.

Alex said nothing of her own suspicions but, once they'd gone, her mind was free to run riot. To her, at least, there was no doubt. She already had reason to suspect Auguste Jalabert of marketing antiques. A dirty, illegal trade, but one which paid well.

There were plenty of avid collectors with no conscience but with money to burn. Why else would Auguste drop such a heavy hint about being interested in anything she might find on an excavation? Certainly Auguste wouldn't have put himself at risk. But could Claude have sneaked in and taken stolen antiquities from that locked office at the hotel? Both father and son had reason to cause Raoul trouble, especially financial loss, causing him to sell . . . to the Jalaberts!

But why try to pass blame on to Alex? And then she remembered Claude's heavy scowl as he spotted her leaving the restaurant at St Cloud . . . with Raoul. She'd avoided saying yes to his own invitation, so revenge would be sweet to a disgusting little slug like him!

The chateau had scarcely opened its

main door the next day when Madame Dupont brought an unexpected visitor as Alex was checking the post.

'Mademoiselle Marthe!' Alex jumped up and went to shake her hand, but Lucie's great-aunt took her by the shoulders and kissed each cheek.

'Alex, I have come to beg your pardon. I am mortified that my sister and Lucie have let you down by their absence. You are tres sympathique and will understand that many emotions need to be overcome before they face the world again. And especially before they face you, my dear.'

'I'll admit to being worried.' Alex prayed Marthe wouldn't guess how much Lucie's outburst was haunting her. She'd agonised over Raoul's reaction, instinctively knowing the girl spoke the truth. Surely he couldn't be in danger of losing the child he'd cherished as his daughter? He wasn't Lucie's father. So who was?

By now Marthe was seated, the morning sun shining through the lozenge-shaped window and turning her white hair to silver.

'Raoul has driven Lucie and my sister Silvie home to La Petite Grotte. It seemed best to take the child back to the place where she was born and has grown up. Its familiarity will help her renew her old relationship with Raoul, who has always regarded her as his daughter.' Sighing a little, she went on. 'Perhaps the truth would have emerged one day. Who knows? But we could never have imagined the distressing way that it came about!'

'That's what I don't understand,' said Alex. 'How on earth did Lucie know?'

'Most unfortunately, by sheer chance Lucie overheard my sister and I talking about Melanie. This was about two years ago. For some reason that I cannot recall we spoke of the woman's death. It happened in America, a car accident when Lucie was only three, and being cared for, here in France, by Raoul. Melanie had told him she must visit her gravely ill mother in Los Angeles. Instead, she was with a man, and he also was killed in the crash. Raoul flew to Melanie's funeral, assuming that she would wish to rest in her family's grave. He discovered that her mother had died many years ago. And that the man was her estranged husband.'

Astonished, Alex was speechless. Poor Raoul!

Marthe read her expression and went on to tell her how Lucie, by then almost a teenager and curious about her mother, had searched Raoul's desk. 'She found a newspaper cutting he brought back from America. It showed photographs of Melanie and the husband.' Turning in her chair, she looked sightlessly into the sky, deep blue beyond the window.

'The man was the image of Lucie — the same broad forehead, the pointed chin, the wide-spaced hazel eyes . . . there could be no doubt!'

Alex had to clear her throat and even

then her voice came out as a hoarse whisper.

'How could Melanie have two husbands at once, one on each side of the Atlantic?'

'Quite easily, I fear! By committing bigamy. By pretending that the baby born seemingly to her and Raoul was premature, whereas in fact it was conceived weeks earlier during a brief reconciliation with the other man. Their relationship was fiery and they parted several times. On one occasion she flounced here, to France and, sadly, met Raoul. He was young and vulnerable, having just lost his father, a strong and seeming invincible man. They 'married' within a month.'

'This is utterly terrible,' said Alex slowly. 'Poor Lucie! And how must Raoul have felt!'

'They deserve your sympathy, especially Raoul. Later he admitted to my sister and me that soon after the so-called wedding he began to feel uneasy. With his father not long in the grave, Melanie had offered to keep the accounts of La Petite Grotte. She was an accountant by profession, so he thought it a natural and kindly thing for her to do.'

'She stole money from the vineyard?'

'Fiddling the books, I believe the English call it.' For the first time Marthe smiled, as though by talking to Alex she felt easier in her own mind.

★   ★   ★

After Marthe left, saying that she would like to return and look around the chateau and its exhibits next week, when the museum and the village returned to normal, Alex forced herself to carry out her everyday routine, though her mind was chaotic. She smiled at interested tourists and told them a little about the medieval years, and as they peered through the glass case and marvelled at the Oriental necklace, she related the story of Marcel and Celestine. When they asked its value, she enjoyed their astonishment on hearing it was beyond price.

It felt good to know everyone was able to enjoy the genuine jewels, even though the replica, normally shown, was — to the layman's eye — identical. Jenna had told her that, even though its stones were only semi-precious, the workmanship involved had been costly. It would have bought a small house, she said. 'But not a big one!'

As usual, Alex went to see that all was well in the snack bar, had a quick coffee there chatting to her helpers, and then made sure that, in turn, the other women on 'guard duty' had a rest and refreshments. She answered questions about the banners and ancient weapons, describing how each Crusader wore a cross on his chest, and an ensign on his lance. And how she longed for the day, the week to end!

Surprisingly, she found herself laughing during the early afternoon. Unexpectedly, the electrician who had worked with Henri when he'd fitted the security system visited with two other young men, not a trio she'd expect to be interested in the long-ago centuries. Greeting them with a smile, she soon found herself chuckling as they poked fun at their old history teacher.

He hadn't done a bad job, she thought privately. They knew an impressive amount, especially about King Richard, his bravery, and his cruelty.

Alex, you're too quick to judge, she scolded herself. They'd been a breath of fresh air on a day she desperately needed some light relief.

An elderly German couple spent a long time poring over the history of the Crusades, painstakingly researched by Alex, and, now set out as a collection of books, paintings and manuscripts in the Library. The woman was in a lightweight wheelchair, thanks to Thomas's wooden entrance ramp. Her white-haired husband steered the chair back into the main hall so they could take a closer look at the necklace.

Alex strolled over to talk to them and

learned that their particular interest arose from the man being a retired jeweller.

'I loved my work but poor eyesight made it impossible once I reached the age of seventy,' he explained. 'The specialists operated on my cataracts but Helga decided it was time for us to travel a little and enjoy ourselves, so here we are! This is wonderful workmanship, fraulein,' he added, nodding towards the glass case.

He didn't look his age, thought Alex, but a smile made most people seem younger. In that case, she must look somewhere near ninety!

As he scrutinised the gold filigree work into which the stones had been set, he launched into an explanation of the means by which Eastern craftsmen would have tackled such an intricate task. His wife began scrabbling in her handbag.

'Helmut, I need my other glasses,' she announced but, fumbling to perch them on her nose, dropped her bag, scattering papers, purse, tourist pamphlets and finally a bag of marble-shaped peppermints. There seemed dozens of them, rolling everywhere as her husband, flustered and embarrassed, muttered 'Helga, why must you carry so much rubbish?'

By now, he and other visitors were chasing them, with his wife issuing instructions from her chair. It was easy to see who was boss, thought Alex mischievously, as she captured one or two of the mints. It was anyone's guess whether they'd have a wash or go back in the handbag! It had been a cheerful few minutes, though, uniting everyone in a good-humoured treasure-hunt.

* * *

On Saturday, the final day of the festival, Mike returned, bringing Bernard and his wife, as well as Nicole. They wandered around the exhibits, saying they'd like to return next week when the chateau was quiet and Alex had promised they could scrutinise more closely some manuscripts which were currently protected by glass.

Alex liked Nicole, and was glad to see how well the young Frenchwoman was getting on with Mike. He was such a nice man, and she'd love to see him happy. There would probably be work for him in France, if they eventually got together as a couple and, if she set her mind to it, Nicole could prove far more attractive than Hadrian's Wall!

'I'll hope we can talk more next week, when you're not so busy, before I trek back to Northumberland,' said Mike just before they left for a last chance to enjoy the market stalls and other attractions beside the river. 'But for now, we'll watch the closing ceremony, and possibly hang around till dark for the fireworks display.'

His face grew serious as he added quietly, 'We've been trying to work out exactly how Raoul's pottery finds went walkabout in the first place. Who did the pinching and who did the receiving?

The police are being mysterious — 'pursuing enquiries' is all they'll say.'

Alex bent to pick up a discarded guidebook and agreed it was a mystery. She had her private thoughts, but it wouldn't be fair to speculate aloud, without proof. As far as her own logic stretched, everything was pointing to the Jalaberts.

Her brow creased as she wondered. If the police or even Bernard's laboratory found some additional clue, how long might it take to nail the pair? And what would happen then?

As for the Giravel family — Raoul and Lucie had many bridges to mend and she could only hope they'd weather this major storm. As for her own relationship with Raoul — if there ever had been one — despite those few words of contrition and plea for forgiveness, could she find it in her heart to forgive and trust him?

15

The final visitor had gone, the main doors were closed, and darkness began to fall at last. Below, along the banks of the river, twinkling lights illuminated the crowds who had come by the busload and an avalanche of cars to enjoy the highlight of St Justin's Week, the firework display.

The fancy dress competition had been judged, prizes awarded and the children, still in their weird and wonderful costumes, were waiting, excited and noisy, for the fun to start.

From the chateau ramparts Alex stood looking across to where the waters of the Dordogne flowed, seamless and dark, towards the sea. Beside her, the marble statue of Celestine stood high, an ethereal figure facing towards the East, watching across the centuries for her Crusader lover to return.

'I hope you're pleased the way things have gone this week,' Alex told the nymph. 'Everyone thought your necklace was wonderful, out of this world, and utterly beautiful!'

She wouldn't be watching the fireworks from the promenade below, preferring to stay near the now-empty chateau tonight. Even Madame Dupont had gone to join her friends and was almost certainly accumulating enough gossip to keep Alex entertained over her morning croissants for the next couple of days.

Earlier, Inspector Vincent had paid another visit, to check final security arrangements for the jewels before they went back to Paris tomorrow. Relieved that the week had passed without incident, he admitted with a reluctant smile that he'd be glad to see the back of them. The firework display could be a distraction, of course, but he had talked again with Henri Lesage about the locking mechanism of the glass display case and was reassured.

Although his officers would have their hands full, especially since some spectators were sure to have brought a few fireworks of their own, Alex was relieved to hear that he'd decided to post one of his men in the shadows beneath the postern entrance. No vehicles were there tonight. Alex confirmed that earlier, Madame Dupont's grocery order had been delivered, but the door was now locked and bolted from the inside.

She was reassured by his visit and especially relieved to know that a policeman was already quietly patrolling the rear of the courtyard, although she hadn't noticed him arrive.

Alex should have felt comfortable. But she wasn't. There was no point in thinking she was being over-fanciful, that the increasingly sombre shadows, the solitude, were the cause of these prickles in her veins. No, it was more than that. Something hadn't been quite right this week. Some small thing. Some very small thing. But what was it?

Nothing she could put a finger on but, all the same, it was there!

Moving closer to the marble nymph, she spoke quietly, even though they were alone.

'Something's wrong, isn't it, Celestine? Can you feel it too?'

The moon hid briefly and then a passing cloud freed a single beam of light. It shone directly on the delicate face above her. Alex reached up to touch the slender ankle.

'Am I being completely neurotic and daft?'

It must have been imagination making the marble feel almost warm. And, strangely, despite the moonlight as clouds parted once more, above her the fragile lines of cheek and brow became shrouded in darkness. Alex frowned. Still the shadows didn't lift.

'You feel it too, don't you?' she whispered, hugging both arms around her body. 'What can I do? They'll think I'm imagining things, feeble even! No one will take any notice if I say 'I've got a feeling!'' Teeth worrying her lower lip, she admitted, 'I'm in a bit of a panic.'

Walking slowly around the statue, at last she came to a standstill. Looking into the night sky, an idea gathered pace.

Should I? Dare I? Am I crazy? Silence enveloped the courtyard and rear of the building, even though she knew the policeman must be there, keeping guard. 'Poor chap,' she muttered, smiling a little at her own foolishness. 'He hasn't even got Celestine to keep him company.' What was he doing? Sitting on the wooden steps leading to the postern gate? Or, eyes and ears alert, slowly patrolling the small, now empty, car park there?

Memory flashed. A cameo incident, something from the week.

That's it! It's all been set up! And I was watching!

Briefly, she wavered, her thoughts racing.

What best to do? Ring for help? For once, her phone was in her pocket.

No. The Inspector would guess her nerves were raw after a hectic week, plus all the work before it had even started. He'd covered all logical possibilities.

What about the policeman at the postern gate? Better leave him on guard. That only left the main door, just behind her. She'd locked it before coming outside. Someone was waiting for the fireworks? A perfect distraction!

Moonbeams flooded the courtyard. Darkness fled. The nymph's face was palest gold and glowing. Alex took one final look and ran up the steps. Unlocking the great door, she fastened it securely once inside. Quickly, she raced upstairs.

★ ★ ★

Less than fifteen minutes later she was back on the terrace, gasping for breath. Just in time! The first shower of coloured stars burst from the promenade, followed by another, and then another. A great cheer drifted upwards.

For almost an hour, wrapped snugly in the anorak she'd grabbed from her office, Alex watched the display, loving the cacophony of stars as they shot in the air, the clouds of red, purple, blue and green steamy light from nearer the ground, and heard each fresh burst of applause from a thousand throats. At last the final, extravagant display of rockets began, signalling what must surely be the end of the carnival.

Shivering despite her jacket, she unlocked the door and went inside. Madame Dupont would be home soon, ready for a coffee before bed. If Alex admitted her extra precautions, the little housekeeper would burst out laughing, and say she was mad.

As the door closed behind her, a massive explosion lit the centre of the great hall. The glass display case shattered into a thousand fragments across the flagstones.

And a heavy blow from behind sent Alex crashing to the floor.

16

Below, on the promenade, Madame Dupont was on a mission. She didn't realise it until she spotted Raoul Giravel standing some distance from the crowd watching the fireworks.

He wasn't with anyone, although she'd sighted Lucie not far away, with a group of other young people. She couldn't see the two aunts anywhere, so perhaps they'd stayed at home, leaving him as Lucie's unwilling chauffeur for the night.

He was near the foot of the winding drive which led to the chateau, leaning against a tree, looking up at the night sky. She had a feeling he wasn't seeing the shooting spangles of light which were drawing oohs and aahs from the onlookers. He seemed lost in his thoughts. Unhappy ones, by the look on his face. *As well they might be,* she thought fiercely, recalling the way he'd thrust past her, up the stairs, shouted at Alex, and stormed out again.

Madame Dupont had become very fond of Alex, as well as being grateful for the help she'd given the de Villiers when they needed her. The housekeeper counted herself as one of that family after serving them for so many years.

Although she'd done her best to hide it, Alex's unhappy eyes betrayed utter desolation since Raoul's bitter attack had left her trembling and fighting to hold back the tears.

The two of them had seemed to be getting on so well, until then! Every time she saw them together, although such moments were few and brief, to Madame it was clear that this was the start of something special. She'd dared to dream of a happy ending, a wedding, and for Alex a life here in St Justin where everyone liked her, admired her spirit, her imagination, the way she'd thrown herself into preparations for this week.

The housekeeper knew only that Raoul's American wife died when Lucie was a toddler, but he'd been a good father. *She's a nice, well-mannered young girl*, she thought, glancing to where the teenager was laughing with her friends, *and best of all, she loves Alex*.

Madame had wondered about Lucie and her aunt's absence these past few days, but thought it best to say nothing. The reason would soon come to light. Not more trouble, she hoped. There had been enough already over those wretched bits of old pot!

Now that Raoul knew Alex was innocent of reporting them, he would surely come and beg her forgiveness? But there'd been no sign of him! He was a proud man, kept his own counsel, and might be regarded as quite distant by anyone who didn't know him. Perhaps he needed courage to admit he was in the wrong.

Madame had seen his eyes light as they looked at her protegee in a way that made her wish she herself was fifty years younger! Not that he'd look at her, of course, but there was no harm in dreaming.

He's still standing there, she mused. *Somehow I need to give him a push. Tell him he should go and see her. Tomorrow!*

Shaking her head, waiting for the answer, she avoided a gaggle of acquaintances ready to swap the latest news. The fireworks would finish soon. Raoul was still leaning against the leafy plane tree, looking as though his thoughts were a million miles away. Or were they only a few hundred yards distant, where Alex was alone in the chateau?

Her strategy decided, the housekeeper made her way across the promenade. Reaching Raoul, she touched his hand. Startled, he looked down and saw her grimacing with pain.

'Monsieur Giravel! I am so glad it is you!' Clutching his arm, she leaned heavily against him. 'Can I beg a little favour?'

'Of course, Madame! How can I help?' If he wished her on some distant planet at that moment, he didn't show it. Surprise was the main emotion on his face.

'I have left my heart pills in my room. And I need them urgently!' Turning from the crowd, now moving towards the river for the final extravaganza, she spoke in a whisper. 'I do not want people to know I have a problem. You know how they will gossip.'

Raoul knew too well how the village news network operated, but already he had an inkling of the favour she was about to ask.

'I saw your vehicle a short distance away. Could you please drive me quickly to the chateau? The crowd is thinner here, and the lane is clear. I will not keep you, so you can return for the end of the display. I see your daughter is safe with friends for the few minutes it will take.'

Not exactly a 'little' favour, thought Raoul dryly, since it probably meant he would need to deliver her safely to Alex. How could he meet her casually, for those few minutes, as though nothing had happened?

He needed hours. Hours to admit how wrong he'd been to doubt her, to beg her forgiveness, to ask for her understanding. That would be the hardest — how on earth could he explain why he'd distrusted her? Why he couldn't believe any woman would commit herself truly and eternally to him?

This had been a terrible week. And, much as he needed time alone with her, this wasn't it — not while she was still working at fever-pitch.

Quickly he fetched his car and helped Madame Dupont into the front seat. She was still clutching her chest and uttering little groans. When he suggested they drive straight to the hospital, she gasped, 'No, No! All I need is one of my tablets. Please, Monsieur!'

Swiftly they reached the courtyard.

As he helped her from the car, the little woman hobbled, still wincing, towards the building. Suddenly she stopped dead. Raoul, following, ready to help her climb the steps, almost cannoned into her.

'Mon Dieu! The door is wide open. Something is wrong!'

She didn't have a chance to move before he rushed past and charged into the hall. She was only seconds behind.

Devastation met their horrified eyes. Shattered glass littered the floor, bunting hung in tatters, the two chain-mailed Crusaders had collapsed amid a jumble of medieval weapons, tapestries and broken ornaments.

The central display, the glass cabinet was in a thousand pieces, the Oriental necklace gone.

Alex lay crumpled and unconscious. Blood trickled across her deathly white face.

Raoul reached her in one long stride. Urgently he felt the pulse at the side of her neck.

'She's still alive. Get an ambulance!' he snapped, his hands carefully feeling Alex's limbs. A mobile phone jutted from her pocket. He thrust it at the housekeeper. 'And get her mother. I need mine to ring the police.' Then, remembering, he glanced at Madame Dupont. 'Are you well enough to do it?'

As she nodded and hurried off, he made the call and then turned back to Alex. She was beginning to stir, her eyelids fluttering slightly.

'Don't move.' His voice was rough, but his touch was gentle, and fear still darkened his face.

'I'm all right,' she whispered, opening eyes filled with pain. 'But I've got a rotten headache!'

'Hush now. Don't talk!'

'You and I aren't talking. Full stop. Have you forgotten?' A weak smile flickered.

'For goodness sake, woman, be quiet!' Relieved, he saw slight movement in her legs and then her arms. 'Keep still.'

Pulling the knotted kerchief from his neck, he carefully wiped blood from her face. Thankfully he saw it came from what seemed to be no more than a flesh wound below her ear.

Already the housekeeper had returned.

'The ambulance is on its way. And so is Madame Graham.'

A flurry inside the entrance brought Inspector Vincent. Swiftly he reached Alex and knelt beside her, hardly glancing to where the jewellery had once dominated the room.

Alex touched his sleeve. 'Please, help me up. I must talk to you.'

He looked dubious but, ignoring him, she started struggling to her feet. Raoul's arms stopped her.

'Where do you want to go?'

'The Library. There's a couch.'

Lifting her with infinite care, he carried her into the other room, followed by the Inspector.

A young policeman entered with news that the guard at the postern entrance had also been attacked. He was wounded, but not seriously. Bludgeoned from behind, he'd regained conscience to find himself bound, gagged and alone.

'I assume the necklace has gone?' Settled on the couch where, unbeknown to anyone, she'd spent each night this week, Alex looked enquiringly at the Inspector.

'I fear so, mademoiselle, but do not worry yourself about it. The important thing is that you are safe,' he reassured her, concern softening his face.

Raoul turned his head towards the main hall, hearing fresh arrivals. 'The ambulance is here.'

'Close the door, Raoul,' Alex told him. 'I must tell you both something.'

He hesitated, then reluctantly did as she asked.

'Did you see or hear anything mademoiselle?' The policeman in Vincent was reasserting itself, though his voice was soft.

'No. But I'd already guessed something was wrong. And Celestine did too.'

'Celestine?' He looked puzzled.

Raoul intervened, body tense, dark eyes stormy and impatient. 'The necklace was a gift for Celestine, an innkeeper's daughter, centuries ago. Her statue stands on the terrace.' His voice was sharp, his violence scarcely contained. 'These wretches tried to kill Alex. She doesn't know what she's saying.'

'Rubbish!' said Alex stoutly, the light of battle sparking her eyes. 'But you can do something for me, apart from making daft comments.'

He subsided, a gleam of white teeth showing amusement, and perhaps relief that, once again, she was fighting him.

'So what is it you wish me to do, Mademoiselle Graham?' he asked politely.

'I'm too hot,' she complained. 'Will you unzip my anorak please?'

His eyebrows lifted but, obediently, he started to tug the zip down from where it sat snugly under her chin.

'What else?'

The fastener moved six inches. His voice trailed into silence. The Inspector jerked forward.

'What . . . ?' The chandelier above them lent iridescent fire to the fabulous necklace clasped around Alex's creamy neck, and hidden beneath the close-fitting jacket.

'I thought it would be safer with me tonight.' The old urchin mischief was back, tempered by a shaft of pain. Briefly her eyes closed.

'Don't talk any more,' commanded Raoul but, lifting heavy lids with obvious effort, she looked at Vincent, a smile hovering around her lips.

'Is this . . . ?' He shook his head, disbelieving. 'Surely it cannot be!'

'It certainly is,' said Alex, her eyes dancing at the sight of their dumb-founded faces.

'Then they have taken . . . what?' he asked, almost lost for words.

'Why, the fake, the replica, whatever you like to call it!'

'Alex,' said Raoul slowly, 'I know you

must leave for the hospital but, for pity's sake, tell us what you've done, how you guessed there would be trouble.'

As she smiled at him, it seemed as if, for this brief interlude at least, they'd both forgotten the anger and hurt which had been tearing them apart.

Carefully, wincing occasionally, she described her increasing unease as the evening wore on. 'Something was niggling at my mind. Some tiny incident from the week that wasn't quite right, something that didn't ring true.'

'And that was . . . ?' her listeners asked, almost in unison.

She looked at the Inspector. 'I started thinking about your officer, the one guarding the postern entrance. I thought he must be feeling bored. Then I wondered if, to break the monotony, he'd stroll around the small car park we'd cordoned off for disabled drivers. And then I knew.'

'Knew what?' This time it was Raoul.

'An elderly German couple had spent

a couple of hours in the museum this week, admiring the necklace. The wife was in a wheelchair. She said she needed her other spectacles and started rummaging inside her handbag. As she pulled out the specs, she accidentally — or so it seemed — sent all the bag's contents flying across the hall. They rolled everywhere. The biggest trouble came from a jumbo-sized bag of peppermints.' A chuckle broke from Alex's lips as she remembered the mayhem it caused. 'They were round, like marbles. All the visitors started scrabbling on the floor, picking them up.' More seriously, she went on. 'Almost certainly the couple had planned the diversion. It gave the husband chance to stick explosive to the underside of the table where the display case stood. No one would have noticed.'

'And a remote detonator could trigger it,' added the Inspector thoughtfully.

'That's right. I'd no idea, of course,

what they'd done. But later, standing beside Celestine's statue, I realised there was every chance they'd been setting everything in place for a robbery.

'I had this overwhelming sense that the necklace would be safer with me. It was a risk but I weighed up the odds and decided to take a chance. I rushed inside, grabbed the replica from the office safe, ran to the cellar and switched off the alarm. Then I shoved the decoy gems in the display case. Finally, a bit out of breath I'll admit,' her mouth curved as she enjoyed their intent faces, 'I closed the cabinet and,' smile widening, 'I wore a fortune under my jacket.'

'Extraordinary!' The Inspector took a long, deep breath. 'So what they have stolen is valueless!'

'Jenna had already told me it might buy a small car — but not an expensive one! I doubt they'll be very pleased when they find out.'

'One more question, and then you

must go,' he said. 'What was it about the car park that made you suspect them?'

'It was Lucie, Raoul's daughter.' For a second, she paused and then, seeing a flicker of emotion cross Raoul's lean cheekbones, forced herself to continue. Unknowingly, her face softened as she explained. 'Lucie has long brown hair and a habit of tossing it back, at the same time doing a sort of light-hearted skip.

'By chance I was looking through a window that overlooks the car park when I saw the husband pushing the wheelchair to their vehicle. You could tell the woman's clothes were expensive, even elegant, and they'd been playing the old-age pensioner parts to perfection. Partly hidden by big horn-rimmed glasses, what you could see of her face was lined, the skin quite pitted. But perhaps vanity wouldn't let her wear a wig. Instead, I'm sure her hair was her own — rather untidy, light brown and tied back with a velvet ribbon.' Alex paused. 'I'm no expert when it comes to fashion. But she needed help with her coiffure!'

She was quiet for a moment and briefly passed a hand across her forehead. Raoul put out his hand as if to touch her, and began to speak but she took no notice. 'Anyway, thinking she was safely beside the car, this 'elderly disabled' woman almost leapt from the wheelchair. Then, tossing back her hair, exactly as I've seen. Lucie do, she gave a little skip as though to say 'Job done!' The man slung the chair in the boot, they jumped in their seats and drove off.'

'Assuredly you are right! We must find these people. But where? They may be in Germany by now, assuming of course that they are German!' The Inspector was thinking hard. 'My team are scouring the hall for fingerprints. Also the postern entrance. They smashed the lock with a small amount of explosive. Nothing was heard, of course, because of the fireworks.'

The door was flung open as Eloise ran into the room. Gathering Alex in her arms, she gently smoothed the dishevelled golden curls.

It was the end of a long day. At last, Alex burst into tears.

⋆　⋆　⋆

Her first visitor at the hospital was Luc. He'd driven overnight from Paris and, hurrying into the small white-walled room, grasped Alex's hands.

'Alex! Thank God you are safe! We would never have forgiven ourselves . . .'

'Luc,' she interrupted. 'What on earth are you doing here? How's Jenna?'

He calmed slightly. 'Jenna is very well, and so is our new daughter.'

'How lovely! But you should be with them!'

'Jenna insists that she has all the support she needs and a husband will only be in the way,' he assured her, his expression easing now he could see

Alex for himself. She was sitting propped against her pillows, pale-faced, a large plaster showing from beneath one ear but, otherwise, looked almost unscathed. 'We can never thank you enough for what you have done, from the moment you arrived in St Justin. But in a million years we couldn't have dreamed we were putting you at such terrible risk!'

Alex reassured him that she was fine, apart from a sizeable bruise on the back of her head and a dull but persistent headache.

'The doctors thought I should stay one more day, although the X-ray showed there's no damage.'

From Luc she learned that the genuine necklace had been returned to Paris by security van, and police were sifting through debris in the hall, fingerprinting and making enquiries. Doubtless the border police would liaise, but the couple would lie low for a while. The hunt was urgent, however, before the necklace could be broken up.

Even though they'd soon realise it was a replica, each gem would still be worth a tidy sum to crooked dealers.

Gertrud, curator at the museum before Alex's arrival, had been in contact with Luc after her mother's recent death, so had returned overnight with him. With a sense of relief, Alex realised that, once the chateau reopened for visitors, she could leave it in the Swiss woman's capable hands.

In the meantime, Alex knew she'd created an exhibition to be proud of. She had often been happy in St Justin, but now it was time to leave. If she left her heart behind — well, no one needed to know.

Luc didn't stay long. He would talk to the police again but planned to drive home the following day, taking Madeleine and Guy with him.

Alex was happy to see him and to relinquish her duties, knowing she'd done her best for the de Villiers family and for the village. She sent love and congratulations to Jenna, but was relieved when he said an affectionate farewell. All she wanted was to close her eyes and sleep.

The medication she'd been given was working and the fierce initial pounding across her temples had lessened. Even so, reaction was setting in and she was glad to be left alone.

Eloise had stayed at the hospital, fending off would-be visitors with her usual charm. There was no need for Alex to feel guilty that Christophe had been abandoned because, said Eloise with a smile, he was enjoying long chats with Philippe at the Auberge des Fleurs, as well as wonderful meals, and almost certainly no lack of wine or cognac!

A second member of the de Villiers family visited because tomorrow, she explained, she must return to Paris with Luc, but was anxious to see for herself that Alex was not seriously injured.

Close to tears, Madeleine, too, expressed heartfelt thanks and apologies for everything that had taken place since Jenna first telephoned to ask Alex's help.

'You've created something that could be the start of a secure future for Guy.' Squeezing Alex's hand, 'There will be a constant flow of visitors looking and admiring it all.'

'After they pay their entrance fee!' added Alex with an unrepentant grin.

'After they pay their entrance fee!' agreed Madeleine, laughing.

When she'd gone, Alex casually mentioned to her mother that, if Raoul Giravel happened to come, she would be willing to see him because she was already feeling so much better. Eloise calmly reassured her that certainly he wouldn't be sent away.

Discreetly, she made no mention of her talk with Philippe and Elspeth at the Auberge des Fleurs. Raoul Giravel's 'Roman pottery' and his confrontation with Alex was still hot village news but absolutely no one believed that Alex, regarded as one of their own, would have tried to make trouble for Raoul.

And now, at last, the truth had come to light. All the police had to do was find who set up the hoax, and why!

There was enormous sympathy for Raoul. Many of the villagers earned their living from working the land, and understood what a setback this had been for him. And all for no purpose, since the archaeologists found absolutely nothing

Alex so wanted to see him but, until he arrived — as surely he would — she lived on the memory of his anxious face as she was lifted into the ambulance. His once-impenetrable black eyes, the strain that showed itself in every line of those lean features, said that he cared for her. But how much? He knew she'd had nothing to do with the pottery, had already accepted her innocence in those few words before he'd had to take Lucie away. In that moment, she'd known that she had reached his heart. But would he listen to it?

By late afternoon, Alex had slept again and was growing restless. Her head still felt as though she'd like to gift it to someone she disliked — anyone — but a coffee and a few biscuits helped.

Eloise came to ask if she felt fit enough for one final visitor — Lucie.

'She is most anxious to see you but only if you agree. I know you are very fond of her.'

Alex had said nothing, even to Eloise, of Lucie's heartbreaking disclosure about her real father. Now her face lit up.

'Lucie! Yes, I'd love to see her.'

Eloise opened the door. Lucie stood, hesitating. As Alex held out her arms she rushed into them, tears streaming down her face. The door closed quietly behind her.

'Hush now, my love,' said Alex, though her own eyes were wet. 'You're taking the starch out of this sexy hospital nightie.'

Lucie raised a tear-stained face, even as a smile began to break through.

'Oh Alex! You are well enough to

make me laugh again. And I love you for it!'

'Well, having got that settled, why don't you sit down and tell me how you are.'

'And I will tell you also about these few days with Papa.'

How much had Lucie guessed about her feelings for Raoul? Alex cautiously asked, 'Papa?'

'Yes.' Lucie's eyes were clear and honest as she met Alex's gaze. 'I have told him that he has always been my father. He always will be my father. No blood tie could be stronger than ours!'

'So all is well between you?'

'He took me home to La Petite Grotte. There, everything is familiar to me because it is where I was born and grew up. We talked and talked, just the two of us.'

'Do you feel able to tell me what he said? Or would you prefer the past to stay private, just between the two of you?'

Lucie shook her head. 'My Aunt

Marthe says that deceit is an uncomfortable bedfellow. The secret of my birth has brought Papa such misery, and troubled my aunts greatly too, of course.' Her smooth brow creased slightly. 'We would not, of course, want others in St Justin to know our private affairs. But you are family and need to know the truth.'

Unspeakably moved, Alex took her hand and held it closely in her own.

'I know I should not have looked inside his desk and found the newspaper cutting. But, you will understand how I needed to know, after my aunts talked about my mother and this unknown man. They had no idea I could hear them!'

'Of course I understand. I'd have been tempted to do the same!'

'Well then, you might say I got what I deserved — more than I bargained for!' Lucie was silent for a moment but then went on. 'It seems my mother was already married to this man but it was a fiery relationship and they split up several times. There was one time when she thought the split permanent, but found she was pregnant. By then she had met Papa.' Her cheeks tinged with pink as she hastily said 'Papa Raoul, that is to say. He was very young and had just lost his father. My mother pretended she was free to marry him.' Fiercely, she muttered, 'That was so wrong! So cruel!'

Alex interrupted, knowing it was important for Lucie to talk but for the girl's sake wanting to reach the end of the wretched tale quickly.

'So you were born and the three of you lived at La Petite Grotte.'

'For almost three years, although Maman returned to America several times because her mother was ill.'

Alex knew she mustn't mention Marthe's disclosure that Melanie's mother had, in fact, died several years earlier. Yet more lies.

'In America that final time, she saw again her real husband.' She shrugged. 'Assuredly, they had arranged to meet, perhaps even continue their marriage! Driving together, they crashed the car. The newspapers there and other people did not know she had another family in France.'

'How do you feel about your mother, now you know more?' asked Alex tentatively, afraid to tread on feelings that must be very sensitive.

'I accept it,' was the surprising answer. 'I remember no hugs, no cuddles. I do not think she wanted children. And, to make up for that, I had my aunts and Papa.'

'One day, might you want to find out more about your biological father?' asked Alex cautiously.

Lucie shrugged her thin shoulders. 'I do not know. Not for a long time anyway. Perhaps never.' Screwing up her face, she ran her fingers through the long brown hair. 'For the moment, I am not even curious. Strange, is it not?'

Alex shook her head and, wincing, regretted it.

'Not really. You've had a lot to

contend with lately. I think the best course of action is to get back to school now that term's started, settle to normal life, and enjoy living with your lovely aunts and the Papa who has known you from the day you were born, and loves you to death!'

Lucie's face broke into the first wide, relaxed smile Alex had seen since happier days when she and Silvie first helped set up their craftwork room.

'You are right.' Her smile faded. 'But Papa has gone.'

'Gone?' Alex's heart plunged. 'What on earth do you mean?'

'He has left us. He has gone away. Aunt Marthe will only say he has gone to the Camargue. She does not know when he will return.'

Somehow Alex managed to keep the shock of this final rejection from showing in her face and her voice. She just expressed mild surprise that he'd left the new vineyard when he'd been so anxious to work according to the moon and its phases. 'But perhaps he still needs a final all-clear from the Ministry of Culture before he starts digging and planting. Or maybe,' grasping at straws, 'there are outstanding problems with the original purchase and finance.'

Lucie seemed ready to agree, and went on to talk about her new teachers and the pressure of impending exams. They'd fallen into the habit of speaking a mix of English and French, as Alex did her best to listen and ask questions, but it was a struggle. All she could think of was Raoul.

Where had he gone, and why? What could be so urgent that it took it away from his passion, the vineyard? He'd been angry with what he saw as her betrayal, and furious that his plans for what was meant to be an exciting new business had been wrecked.

If his timetable was no longer so vital, why hadn't he come to talk to her? She'd seen strong, raw emotion in his face, and felt it in the security of his arms when he'd carried her to the ambulance. Surely he would at last admit to feelings that had increasingly often lit his harsh face with warmth and charm?

Alex knew it was time to pull down the final curtain. She'd fallen head over heels in love with a man who could never commit himself, or trust, a woman. He might love her, might long for her with a scarcely leashed masculinity that made her tremble, but he'd never want a permanent relationship. A brief affaire — yes — but that would be a bitter harvest. What she wanted, and longed for, was complete love and trust . . . something he wouldn't give.

Lucie kissed her and said an affectionate au revoir. Alex waited for the door to close, then pushed aside the bedclothes. By the time her mother entered, she was almost dressed.

Ignoring Eloise's dismay, she said, 'I'm well enough now, Maman. I want to go home. To Aix.'

Eloise's arguments fell on ears determined not to hear. An hour later they were gathering Alex's belongings from the chateau, and saying farewell to Madame Dupont.

'Soon you will come back to us,' said the little woman anxiously, disconcerted by the speed of what was happening.

'I'm sure St Justin will call me,' said Alex evasively, knowing she would never return. The village had brought such happiness, offered her a golden future and then snatched it away.

★ ★ ★

She stayed overnight at the Auberge des Fleurs but by dawn, with Eloise and Christophe, she was on her way south to Aix-en-Provence. Christophe claimed he'd been longing to drive the tiny blue car, since Eloise insisted Alex wasn't yet fit.

'It reminds me of my student days,' he'd joked, quiet amusement in his face. 'I will trust your mother with my own car. And I'll expect the pair of you to leave it sparkling!'

They broke their journey at Villeclos, as Alex had done before, but left early and by mid-afternoon had arrived at Eloise's home on the beautiful road to Le Tholonet, below Cezanne's famous and much-painted grey mountain.

Alex had spoken to Mike by telephone, grateful that he asked no questions but accepted her longing to get away from St Justin for a while at least. He and Nicole would have another good look around the museum and particularly the delicate manuscripts. Then he, too, must leave.

He said something else to make her wonder if he would return fairly soon. Apparently a major new excavation was about to begin in the Dordogne and he was tempted to join the team.

'It'll give me a chance to see more of Nicole.' he added offhandedly, 'Though I'd still keep in touch with whatever's going on in dear old Hadrian's patch!'

Alex had smiled, although a shadow clouded her eyes. She was getting used to being dumped. Shaking herself, she genuinely hoped things would go well with Mike and Nicole. As for herself, desolation was no stranger. She'd do well to set a match to crazy imaginings when it came to a proud, dark-eyed man who belonged in the wide open spaces.

17

The sun was shining across the wide, busy squares and sparkling fountains of Aix-en-Provence but there was no brightness in Alex's heart.

This morning, relieved to be at home again, she'd driven into the centre of Aix, squeezed into a cramped parking spot on the Rue Cardinale and walked through narrow streets to Le Tomate.

Eloise had been obliged to go to the university and prepare some additional teaching materials for the autumn term, but suggested that she and Alex meet for lunch in town.

'You could have coffee while you're waiting, cherie. The bistro won't be busy mid-morning and I know it's one of your favourite haunts.'

Alex said nothing. Could she bear a return to the place where she'd first met Raoul and Lucie? Then she told herself not to be so pathetic. It was time to face painful memories, and she liked the bistro. That was all that mattered!

Now, she waited for her coffee, and then perhaps there'd be time for a stroll around the market before meeting Eloise. As usual, she sat reading a book until a shadow fell across the page and a voice asked, 'Pardon, mademoiselle. May I share your table?'

A sideways glance showed plenty of free spaces. Frowning slightly, she looked up, her pulses rioting as she met achingly familiar, slightly quixotic eyes.

'Raoul!' Struggling for breath, 'What are you doing here?'

'Hoping for coffee, and then perhaps,' he was uncharacteristically hesitant, 'A chance to talk and even have lunch with you.'

'I'm meeting my mother for lunch . . .' Even as the words left her mouth, Alex wondered if she was dreaming. He couldn't be here! Why was he here? How did he know she'd be here, at this place, at this hour?

As if she'd said it all aloud, he answered. Already the skinny black-clad waitress had brought his coffee, black and hot. Had she poured it the moment he walked through the door? When it came to masculine appeal, Raoul Giravel left every other man standing. Today he'd discarded the formal business suit he'd worn on that first occasion, and was dressed in grey slacks and the suede jacket she'd seen before. Unusually, he wore a tie with his white shirt.

'Your mother suggested I should take her place. I had telephoned, hoping that you wouldn't slam down the receiver!' Briefly he smiled. 'She told me you would be here and thought perhaps you wouldn't mind. She knows we have a lot to discuss.' He stretched a long arm across the table and gently closed Alex's book, again smiling faintly as he read the title. 'More Mary Stewart and more Merlin, I see. I wondered if your unhappy experience in St Justin would have turned you away from history.' His mouth tightened. 'It seems that I am wrong. Your mother tells me you plan to travel to Egypt very soon.'

Alex found her voice at last, desperate to hang onto a scrap of pride. It was a comfort to know she might not be looking as wretched as she'd been feeling. Her deep blue sleeveless blouse echoed the colour of her eyes and white cut-off jeans showed tanned ankles that Jenna once joked she'd give her eye teeth to own.

'Yes, I'll be off to the East quite shortly. I've applied to join the new excavation. I know others who'll be there, so we'll have fun as well as a fascinating dig.'

'You would not want to miss it?' His expression was intent, as though straining to find something deeper behind her deliberately light tone.

'No reason to,' she said briskly. 'My mother and Christophe get along so well that I reckon they'll move in together soon. So she won't need me around all the time. In any case, I can't live on fresh air — I need a job.'

'There may be others keen to keep you fed and clothed but, naturally of course, they couldn't offer Egypt's excitement.' Impatiently, he drained his cup, lifted a finger for the bill and paid for Alex's coffee too. 'We must talk, but not here.' Pushing back his chair, he extended a hand. 'Will you come with me? Please?'

Nodding, but avoiding his touch, Alex followed him to the door. As though in a trance, she walked beside his tall figure, across the market square, and along a street to where the familiar black saloon was parked.

Without words, they drove a few miles from town. Eventually he stopped in a place where, in the dusty russet-red soil, a narrow pathway led upwards beneath spreading green umbrella pines.

In silence they walked towards the lower mountain slopes, where tumbled grey rocks lay in profusion, their colours intensified by a sky of azure blue. Reaching for her hand, he tugged her gently the last few metres to where a small plateau overlooked the scattering of trees.

Neither had spoken since leaving Aix and now, although Raoul had said they must talk, he seemed reluctant to begin.

In the end it was Alex who prompted him.

'Lucie told me you'd gone away. She didn't know where you were, or when you planned to return.' He said nothing and after a moment she risked asking, 'Is everything all right?'

He relaxed at last and, as she perched on an outcrop of boulders, wandered a few paces to stare into the distant haze before swinging back to face her. Although she could see strain on his face, there was something different about him, as if the shield which had once held him distant, remote, had fractured.

'Everything is very all right. And I will tell you where I have been. But firstly there are so many apologies and explanations I must make you that I don't know where to start.'

'Well, how about at the beginning?' suggested Alex. 'We were getting to know and,' she dared a glance at him, 'perhaps even to like each other.'

At last, amusement creased the lean cheeks. 'You could describe it in that way, I suppose.'

She wasn't going to get much help from him, so she decided to confront him head on.

'Then came the Roman remains fiasco. Antiquities supposedly found on your land by me and sneakily taken to the police.'

'Yes.' For a moment he frowned heavily, staring at the ground, but then raised his head to look directly into her eyes, his own reflecting deep remorse. 'I'm ashamed beyond words that, for a while, I believed the lie. My only excuse is that I'd believed that at last I had found someone special, someone to trust. It took time to break through the defences of years that I'd built around myself, and to believe you were true. You would never deliberately cause me harm. I can only hope that, in time, you will forgive me.'

'Never mind that,' she said impatiently. 'I've heard from the museum authorities that they've traced the origins of the pots.'

'Yes. We were fortunate in that international police recently arrested a man who had a criminal record for trading in stolen antiquities. After release from prison last year, he'd returned to his undercover business. One particular trail led to St Justin and Auguste Jalabert.'

When Alex showed no surprise, Raoul raised an enquiring eyebrow. 'You guessed?'

'Straight away,' she admitted. 'But it wasn't right to point a finger without any proof. He'd already tried to recruit me because, of course, my job meant I sometimes found things which might be of value. Said he had contact with private collectors.' She thought for a moment. 'Did that nasty little snake Claude pinch the pieces from Auguste's office? His dad kept it scrupulously locked — which struck me as rather over-cautious. After all, the holiday season had hardly started when he hauled me in for one of his special chats. There wouldn't have been much cash around.'

'One of Claude's gambling circle gave him away. Claude had promised to pay the man if he'd leave the box of fragments outside a police station one quiet night. He lived in Cahors, which is why it was found there. Your 'nasty little snake' didn't part with the money, and already owed him a tidy sum, so the end was inevitable.'

'What will happen now?'

'The Jalaberts are no longer in St Justin and the hotel is being put on the market. No one is sorry to see them go. Claude is in trouble for wasting police time and,' he gave a brief, humourless laugh, 'he will certainly need to hide from his creditors. Auguste has been charged with handling stolen goods. He's likely to face a prison sentence.'

'Serves him right, the toad!'

A smile tugged at the corner of Raoul's mouth, though his lean face was perplexed.

'My only query is why Claude should try to lay suspicion on you.'

Alex flushed but faced him with clear eyes.

'He tried to date me and I put him off. Then he saw me with you at the restaurant in St Cloud.'

He sighed. 'That explains much.'

'It was ridiculous for him to feel angry. It was only dinner, for goodness' sake!'

As soon as the words left her mouth, Alex wished them unsaid. Turning her head away, to concentrate on a butterfly-which alighted on a frond of wild thyme nearby, she remembered the rest of that magical evening.

Raoul was obviously remembering too. He came closer to where she was sitting, her hair brilliantly golden in the afternoon sun. Reaching out, as though unable to help himself, he touched a burnished curl and let it wind around his finger, as he had once before. Then, sitting beside her, he captured both her hands and held them tightly.

'I am so very sorry. For everything!' He added quietly, 'But not for our very special evening together.' Dark, penetrating eyes searched her face but when Alex said nothing, her gaze moving from the butterfly to focus on a feathery tuft of cloud, he released her, stood, moved back a few paces and, hands in pockets, faced her.

'When I brought Lucie to the chateau that day and she accused me of deception, that she knew I wasn't her father, your face reflected my own utter, soul-shaking horror.' Pausing, his face sombre, after a moment he continued. 'More than that, I knew you felt my agony — that the family life I'd built for her had suddenly shattered.' His voice was so low that she had to strain to hear. 'You will find it hard to believe but, even before that terrible moment, I knew in my heart that you'd never want to hurt me. Every instinct cried that I could trust you!'

'So many truths coming into the light as we stood there with the marble nymph,' reflected Alex, almost to herself, remembering the scene, a frozen tableau. 'She, too, paid a heavy price for hidden secrets.'

He inclined his head, understanding.

'Your friend Celestine also had no trust! If only she'd waited, she would have found that Marcel was true to her.'

'Well, at least she made sure the German couple didn't pinch her necklace,' said Alex with a flash of humour. 'She certainly transmitted some pretty intense feelings to me that night! Did Inspector Vincent tell you those wretches have been traced? By sheer good luck, when the woman tipped her handbag clutter everywhere we all scrabbled to pick it up, but missed a lipstick. It skidded behind one of the Crusaders and tucked itself in a crack on the floor. There were two clear fingerprints, which matched some already on police files. And dear old Helmut and Helga had no time to sell the necklace. Though any jewellery fence would have spotted it was a fake. I'd love to see their faces if that had happened!'

A peal of laughter lit her face to the delicate beauty which had always entranced him.

'Luc rang to tell me the replica is back inside a brand new display case in the main hall. Although the tourist season's reaching its end, the chateau is still attracting plenty of visitors.'

Raoul was silent. Hands jammed in the pockets of his dark grey trousers, he seemed intent on looking through the trees to where, below, the narrow road wound past a few creamy homesteads to the lavender fields beyond.

Alex didn't hurry him. She knew it wasn't the old, uncommunicative silence from their earliest meetings, but his struggle to move on to other, vital revelations. At last he turned to face her.

'Lucie will have told you that we talked for hours, days even, and she accepts that I had no alternative — I couldn't be cruel enough to tell her about her parents. She was relieved the truth is now in the open. It made me wonder if other truths might still be hidden.'

Hands still thrust in his pockets, he compressed his lips as if reluctant to speak those truths aloud. But then, dark brows drawn together, he went on.

'I confronted Marthe and Silvie. I insisted on knowing what happened between my parents during their marriage. My aunts didn't want to talk, saying it was so many years ago, but I demanded the truth. Finally they realised, reluctantly, that I must learn how it had been. Only then was there any chance of my life moving on.'

His voice roughened.

'I should explain that my father was a good parent and materially I was well

cared for. Emotionally, however . . . '
He threw one arm out towards the
horizon, his expression suddenly bleak.
'There was nothing. No softness, no
companionship, no feeling. He was a
hard man, one who should never have
had the care of a motherless boy.'

This time the silence was longer.
Alex ventured a question, though she
scarcely dared to breathe in case she
broke the thread that was letting him
reveal so much.

'What did your aunts tell you?'

His smile was mirthless. 'That for
years they had remained loyal to my
father, their only brother. They said the
scene had been played out with other
women before my mother came, but
she was the one he married. As soon as
he'd installed her in his house, she
became virtually a prisoner. He was
wildly jealous, suspicious, accusing her
of bizarre assignations with workmen,
shopkeepers, even bus drivers. She was
a pretty girl, lively, but faithful. My
aunts saw her rarely but noticed how

she became very quiet, even timid.

'When I was born, matters grew worse. My father insisted our groceries were delivered to the house, that she never went to town unless he accompanied her. He arranged for a hairdresser to come to their home each month, and his two labourers were elderly men who could hardly lift an axe, let alone seduce a young woman.'

Alex, listening, watched dismayed as lines of misery engraved his cheeks. She knew his imagination was seeing his mother and her gradual realisation that she was trapped.

'Things came to a head when I was five, and old enough to attend nursery school. My father was called away on business for two days. My mother gathered courage, ignoring his instruction that she keep me at home. Instead, she drove into the village each morning — she could scarcely remember how to change the gears — and collected me each afternoon. When he found out, he went to the school, and found that the head teacher was a man.'

Running both hands through his black curls, he seemed to have forgotten that Alex sat listening. Although he stared intently above the gently moving branches, she knew he saw, not trees, but his own thoughts. Swinging back to her, he was clearly struggling to continue.

'My father came home in such a passionate rage that finally my mother realised his jealousy was a sickness, an obsession she hadn't the knowledge or strength to fight. One option was to stay with him and become a shadow. Her other choice was to leave. But if she went, and took me, my father would follow. He would never relinquish his son.'

Raoul's tone was bitter. 'The woman who had been his faithful, loving wife was free to leave — as far as he was concerned, there were plenty more available.'

'But he didn't bring another woman home?'

'No, thank the fates. The vineyard was a perpetual struggle, a five-year-old son a time-consuming responsibility. The solution came when my Aunt Marthe was suddenly widowed. She and Silvie offered to live with him, and look after his child — me.'

'And they've said nothing, for all these years?'

He shook his head.

'No, they were excessively loyal to their brother. It is only recently, Marthe admitted, they began to question that loyalty.' His dark eyes were direct. 'When you came into our lives.'

A tremor in her voice was the only sign that Alex heard those last few words.

'Did they know where your mother went when she ran away?' she asked.

'Not at first. But they heard from her after my father's death. She was concerned that I might be alone.' His face hardened. 'It would have been better for me if I had stayed alone, but they told her I had recently married and my wife was expecting a child — Lucie.'

Raoul's unexplained, sudden absence after the chateau robbery was starting to become clear.

'You've been looking for your mother?'

His teeth gleamed in a sudden, almost joyous smile. 'Yes. And found her.'

'She's well? Was she pleased to see you?'

'Very happy. She remarried after my father's death — she hadn't dared contact him earlier, even to request divorce. My aunts thought she was living in the Camargue, where she was born and had friends, so it wasn't hard to find her.'

'And you talked.'

Throwing back his head, he laughed. 'I needn't tell you how many hours we have talked. She'd known people who confirmed that, as a young boy, I was well cared for by my aunts but, even after my father's death, she thought it too late to come back into my life. She believed I might have been brought up to hate her.'

'Instead of which,' dared Alex, 'you fell into Melanie's snare.'

He lifted his hands expressively. 'Fool that I was! There's no excuse except for my youth, and my father's death. Suddenly this beautiful young woman came along.' He grinned, letting Alex glimpse the innocent youth he'd been at that time. 'And she offered to do my accounts — how could I resist!'

'So you put her on the La Petite Grotte payroll,' added Alex, trying to ignore a shaft of jealousy, unwilling to imagine him with another woman.

'Yes. Again such a fool!'

'Forgive me for saying this,' said Alex slowly after a few moments as she studied the straps of her white leather sandals, 'I'm delighted that you've been reconciled with your mother. And that you and Lucie are probably closer than you've ever been. But I can't grasp why you seem so relaxed now about leaving your new vineyard at St Justin and the

306

ultra-strict timetable you were adamant must be followed. After all, that's partly why you were in such a rage when you accused me over the Roman stuff!'

Unable to stay still any longer, she jumped up and went to the edge of the narrow plateau. Then, turning almost violently on Raoul, she flung out both arms in complete exasperation.

'Why are you wasting time here in Aix?' Without warning, the hurt that had been festering inside her heart these past weeks burst into bitter words. Her desolation was still there, beneath the surface. Even though he was here, in front of her. Why had he come?

'Have you taken a couple of hours away from your grapes to shout at me again while you're down south?' Sarcastically, 'Oh, I forgot. You've decided to stop off and buy me lunch.'

Raoul understood. Coming closer, he took her hand and drew her to where she'd been sitting on the grey boulder. Again, he sat beside her.

'I deserve your anger, and your doubts. I've treated you more cruelly than anyone could imagine!' With a tiny tug he pulled Alex towards him and lifted her chin with a gentle hand. 'After all those things, how could you know that being here with you here, and praying that you understand, is more important than anything in the world?'

When she didn't respond, he added wryly, 'And, to make you really believe that, I'm — as the English might say — scraping the bottom of the financial barrel!'

His laugh was unexpected and so lighthearted that she blinked, wondering if she was imagining all this — the sunshine, the beautiful scenery, and most of all Raoul being here.

'You and I have more friends in St Justin than either of us realised, and the leader is Madame Dupont! She realised the village's disgust that men born in their own community had played such evil tricks.'

'The Jalaberts?'

He nodded. 'There's a strong suspicion that Auguste fed into Claude's silly head the idea of somehow sabotaging my plans for the Dessart vineyard and house. He guessed my finances were stretched to the limit, so what better way to force me to sell than by causing serious delay? I couldn't even have worked the vines left by Dessart. Having driven me out, they'd have bought the land that reaches the river.'

'So what has Madame Dupont done?' she asked wonderingly.

'She mobilised some retired men — labourers, builders and suchlike to help me for a few hours daily. She reminded them of their debt to you, my lovely Alexandrie, for the work you put into helping create a grand festival week. She pointed out, too, that a new, successful vineyard would bring prestige to the village. So work is going ahead on the land, and repairs on the Dessart homestead. Soon it will be ready for a new family.' Pausing briefly, his gaze intent, 'My family.'

'Oh.' Not daring to analyse what he meant, Alex couldn't bring herself to look into his face. 'That's wonderful!' Wrinkling her forehead. 'I know this sounds inquisitive, but how on earth will you finance an army of workers?'

'As long as I pay for materials, all they ask is a grand party, perhaps at harvest time each year. They and Madame Dupont insist I'm doing them a favour, a project they'll enjoy. Above all, though she'd never admit it, she can run loose on what she calls 'a bunch of useless old men'!'

At last Alex gave a peal of laughter. 'Oh, you're right! She'll be in her element!'

'She'll only be content when she hears the rift between you and me is mended. And so,' his voice deepened, 'I need first of all to say that I love you.'

'You love me?' she echoed, not sure she'd heard him correctly.

'I fell in love with you here, in Aix, the day I came to buy the Dessart property.' He took her hands again.

'There was an instant spark between us. I dare to hope you felt it too.' Heavy brows contracting, he cast a sideways look at her serious face. 'But then commonsense, and the fact of Lucie, meant I should keep away. She grew so fond of you, there could be no question of a casual affaire. Even if you agreed!' Ruefully, 'Of the sort I'd once or twice tried before. My only excuse for such — 'brief encounters' — is that I had never shaken off the past.'

Quickly she said, 'But you've put that right. You know the truth. Your mother didn't abandon you.'

'Yes. I know finally how wrong I was to believe she and Melanie came from the same mould. Where Melanie is concerned I was a gullible young fool and deserved to be cheated. You know how efficiently she managed it!'

'So, what next?' she asked, not daring to meet the eyes watching her so intently.

He hesitated. 'Above all, I want you to love me and to marry me, live with me, and raise a family with me.' He fell silent and Alex could tell that he was struggling to put his next words together. She waited, even though she wanted to throw herself in his arms and say she'd loved him since the dawn of Time, and her answer was 'Yes, yes, yes!' But he hadn't asked the vital question yet.

Instead, he suddenly said, 'I talked with your friend, Mike.'

What now? Wide-eyed, she stared at him.

'I can't marry until I've proved that you need not be afraid.'

'Afraid? What on earth are you talking about? Afraid of what?'

'Of me! Afraid that I've inherited my father's jealousy, possessiveness, what would nowadays be classed as capacity for mental cruelty.'

Her heart wept for his uncertainty, now he knew the reality of the man who had fathered and reared him.

'Oh Raoul, I'll accept that we still haven't spent much time together, but I know all those dreadful things are alien to you!'

He inclined his head, again pushing back the unruly curls in a way that was endearingly familiar.

'Thank you, my wonderful Alex. But I must first prove it to you.'

'How?' she whispered. Surely she wasn't going to face more heartache?

'Mike told me he's thinking of joining an excavation in the Dordogne area, not too far from St Justin.' He grinned. 'Nor from Nicole!' As Alex smiled, understanding, he said, 'If you would live with me, firstly at the Huillier cottage and then, as soon as it's habitable, we could move into the former Dessart house, you could go to the dig each day. If the travel proved too much, you could lodge there, but come home to me each weekend. Please.'

He'd taken her breath away. Reading her silence as uncertainty, his eyes grew anxious.

'It would mean you staying in

France, and not going to Egypt. But, if your heart is set on that, I can wait.' His lips quirked as, ruefully, he admitted, 'I'd find that hard, but it would give you time to think. And that is essential!'

Alex, her vivid eyes filled with love, moved closer, her hands moving down his cheeks and tracing the carved line of his jaw.

'You're quite some man, Raoul Giravel! Did no one ever tell you that?' Reaching up, she kissed his lips slowly, feeling his response. It was hard to break away. 'I love you and I would love to marry you, without waiting longer than it takes to buy Lucie a brides-maid's dress! But if it makes you happier, let's do as you suggest.' Frowning, she continued, 'Although living 'out of wedlock' might raise a few eyebrows in St Justin.'

'Not in these modern times,' he reassured her. 'In fact, I mentioned the possibility to Marthe. To reassure her. She and Silvie would love you to be one of our family, but knows how little time we've had together. You'll find this hard to believe, but she said I should 'talk around the subject' with Madame Dupont.'

'Good heavens! How extraordinary!'

'We seem to have formed an alliance since you were attacked. And you don't yet know about her trick with the heart pills.'

'Heart pills? I'd swear she doesn't take any!'

'Quite so!' Raoul flung back his head and laughed. 'Anyway, the lack of pills forced me to take her to the chateau that night.'

Seeing Alex's puzzled expression, he explained, enjoying her giggles. Then, again, he reminded her, 'We've had little time together, much of it wasted. She has faith that I would treat you well and the village would be happy.'

Now, at last, he relaxed, smiling, and for the first time Alex saw how happiness made him younger than his years.

'I reckon she and I need to have a

little chat,' she chuckled. She would have entrusted her life to him without question. But, sensitively, she knew Raoul to be a proud man, who needed to prove to himself as much as to her, that he'd inherited no trace of his father's personality.

One eyebrow raised, he said, 'There is still one vital question. Will you choose Egypt? Or me?'

Alex didn't hesitate. She threw her arms around his neck as his own closed almost fiercely and yet tenderly, around her slim body. As his mouth, firm and warm and hard met hers, she knew the future was theirs.

*　　*　　*

Two years later Alexandrie Giravel sank, breathless, into a cane garden seat beside Raoul's mother, Marie. Earlier, two long trestle tables laden with food had been set out in the shady courtyard under leafy fig trees and a festive crowd had eaten and drunk, with plenty of laughter and a few speeches, especially a heartfelt thank you from Raoul.

Marie would spend a few days here with her husband, Justin, to celebrate the harvest of grapes from the original Dessart vines, which thrived this year. In another twelve months, Raoul hoped everyone would be sampling the results of his experiments with biodynamic vine growing, the centuries-old rhythm which moved in tune with the lunar calendar. If all went well, his venture would meet the standards internationally recognised for this new vintage and even open a worldwide market for it.

Alex had liked Raoul's mother the instant they met at her home in the Camargue. It was easy to see the likeness between mother and son — the dark curly hair, and equally dark eyes. There the likeness ended because Marie was a bubbly little woman, who was an instant hit with Lucie as well.

Both had witnessed Alex and Raoul's wedding a year ago, Lucie wearing a bridesmaid's dress of blue silk, her eventual choice just as Alex, Marthe and Silvie were beginning to despair.

'Cherie, you simply cannot go to a wedding in T-shirt and jeans — and that is what will happen if you don't make up your mind!' Silvie had tried to sound strict.

The chapel at the chateau was too small for more than a handful of relatives and close friends, but a few weeks later Eloise arranged a special celebration in Aix-en-Provence, so that all Alex's family could share the happiness she'd found with Raoul.

For much of the first year Alex had worked at a new excavation in the Dordogne region, alongside Mike and Nicole. She and Raoul were delighted to attend their marriage that winter.

Mike soon settled into working in France, although he kept in touch with colleagues in the north of England. He'd become a favourite with his new family here. Once or twice, after an exceptionally heavy day, Alex stayed with them, near the dig, but was always keen to get home to Raoul — firstly at the Huilier cottage, but then at what had once been old man Dessart's house.

Roof, electrics and plumbing were soon renewed. Then she'd revelled in converting the rooms, to make it an inviting, comfortable home.

Raoul was loving, fair and thoughtful. She'd known he would be, but had to accept that he must prove it to himself. During that first year, she delighted in seeing him visibly relax. Gone was the remote, enigmatic stranger of those early days when they'd first met in Aix. Now he smiled readily, and seeing his dream of a new vineyard come to life with Alex beside him, he seemed a different man. And one she loved even more.

Sometimes they'd disagree on minor issues, but agree to compromise. At other times Raoul would deliberately provoke her and await a fiery response. More often than not, she'd see the glint in his eye and subside in giggles. It was the deeply affectionate, romantic partnership she'd always dreamed of but never expected to find.

Pierre, Raoul's manager at La Petite Grotte, could be relied on to keep that vineyard in good health. Marthe and Silvie still lived there with Lucie, but sometimes drove the short distance to St Justin. Raoul went each week to consult Pierre, and often brought Lucie back for the weekend and short school holidays. In autumn she would start college and then, hopefully, study at university in Paris, with Jenna and Luc close at hand.

Today they were here with their children, Michel and Rosa, an enchanting toddler with Luc's dark hair but Jenna's grey eyes. Relieved that, again this summer, the chateau had proved a magnet for tourists, the de Villiers family were cautiously optimistic about the future.

As Alex sat talking with Marie, Justin came to ask if they would like another drink. They were well-matched, thought

Alex. Justin stocky and reliable, but with a sense of humour that responded to Marie's liveliness now the constraints of those wretched early years had left her for ever.

Raoul strolled from where he'd been talking to Madame Dupont and some of his helpers from the village. Lucie was with him. As Alex looked up, smiling, he took her hand and kissed it lightly.

'Lucie is wondering if you'll go riding with her tomorrow,' he said. 'She wants to look for Iron Age knives.'

Playfully, Lucie punched his shoulder.

'I want no more jokes from you, Papa! Just wait until I'm an eminent historian. People will pay good money to come and hear my lectures!'

He tried to look repentant. 'I beg your pardon, mademoiselle!' His eyes travelled over Alex's happy eyes and her face, tanned not from Eastern sun but from hours on the French archaeology project and in the vineyard, where she enjoyed working alongside her husband.

'Have you a moment to spare, Madame Giravel? Jacques Cours has a small boat which you need to see. We might find it useful, and he's not asking much for it.'

Alex rose, telling Marie she would soon return and, linking her hand in Raoul's walked a couple of hundred metres to where the river meandered before it turned away to flow downstream. Standing on the grassy bank, shielded by a leafy wall of their new vines, she looked around.

'I can't see a boat.'

'That's because there isn't one. We need to go and look at it in his yard tomorrow.'

'Then why . . . ?'

'You're in great demand, and I'm happy all our guests are here.' Raoul's voice deepened as he touched the bright curls. 'But I want to be alone with you, just for a few minutes.'

'Well, how d'you plan to spend those

minutes?' she asked with a sly upward glance. 'We're alone now!' Fleetingly her hand touched the almost imperceptible curve below her waist. *But we won't be for long!*

★   ★   ★

Inside a huge Paris museum, hundreds paused as they wandered, and marvelled at the intricate gold filigree that secured each glistening jewel in the Oriental necklace, Marcel's gift of love.

In the village of St Justin, as the River Dordogne flowed smoothly between its banks, from the chateau ramparts Celestine, the marble nymph, smiled.

1967: Upon her death, Lucie Curtis's mother leaves behind a letter that sends her reeling — she was adopted when only a few days old. Soon Lucie is on her way to France to find the mother who gave birth to her during the war. But how can you find a woman who doesn't want to be found? And where does Lucie's adoptive cousin, investigative journalist Yannick, fit in? She is in danger of falling in love with him. However, does he want to help or hinder her in her search?

SURFING INTO DANGER

Ken Preston

All Eden wants to do is roam the coast surfing, at one with the waves and her board, winning enough in competitions to finance her nomadic lifestyle. But first the mysterious Finn, and then a disastrous leak from a recycling plant, scupper her plans. With surfing out of the question, Eden investigates. As the crisis deepens, who can she trust — and will she and her friends make it out alive from Max Charon's sinister plastics plant?

HIS DAUGHTER'S DUTY

Wendy Kremer

Upon her father's death, Lucinda Harting learns that she faces an impoverished future unless she agrees to marry Lord Laurence Ellesporte, who reveals that his father and hers had made the arrangement in order to amalgamate the two estates. For her sake and that of the servants, she accepts, though they live mostly separate lives. Until one day when shocking news reaches Lucinda's ears: Laurence has been arrested as a spy in France! Determined to secure his release, she heads to Rouen with Laurence's aunt Eliza, and a bold plan . . .

SUMMER OF WEDDINGS

Sarah Purdue

Claire loves her job as a teacher, but always looks forward to the long summer break when she can head out into the world in search of new adventures. However, this summer is different. This summer is full of weddings. When Claire meets Gabe, a handsome American in a black leather jacket and motorbike boots, on the way to her best friend Lorna's do, she wonders if this will be her most adventurous summer yet. Will the relationship end in heartache, or a whole new world of possibilities?

LOVE CHILD

Penny Oates

Knowing she was adopted, Lara was nevertheless happy with the parents who brought her up. But when she accidentally discovers her birth parents, she is catapulted into a life completely alien to her — and comes up against the insurmountable obstacle that is Dominic Leigh. She can't understand why he seems determined to keep her away from her father, or why he suspects her of wanting to cause trouble. She vows to overcome his interference, and in doing so, finds so much more than she had bargained for . . .

A MATCH FOR THE FOOTMAN

Gail Richards

It's 1844, and housemaid Emma's life of toil in Lewin Hall is brightened by the arrival of handsome new footman Thomas. When Emma is given an opportunity, along with Thomas and a few others, to work without supervision restoring a neglected house, they relish the freedom and responsibility. But malign influences are at work. As Emma fights to make sense of events, will she be able to protect everything she holds dear — and will her and Thomas's love survive all they have to face?

SPECIAL MESSAGE TO READERS

THE ULVERSCROFT FOUNDATION
(registered UK charity number 264873)
was established in 1972 to provide funds for
research, diagnosis and treatment of eye diseases.
Examples of major projects funded by
the Ulverscroft Foundation are:-

- The Children's Eye Unit at Moorfields Eye Hospital, London
- The Ulverscroft Children's Eye Unit at Great Ormond Street Hospital for Sick Children
- Funding research into eye diseases and treatment at the Department of Ophthalmology, University of Leicester
- The Ulverscroft Vision Research Group, Institute of Child Health
- Twin operating theatres at the Western Ophthalmic Hospital, London
- The Chair of Ophthalmology at the Royal Australian College of Ophthalmologists

You can help further the work of the Foundation
by making a donation or leaving a legacy.
Every contribution is gratefully received. If you
would like to help support the Foundation or
require further information, please contact:

THE ULVERSCROFT FOUNDATION
**The Green, Bradgate Road, Anstey
Leicester LE7 7FU, England
Tel: (0116) 236 4325**

website: www.ulverscroft-foundation.org.uk